THE SEA GULLS ARE CALLING

Published by Paloma Books
(An imprint of L&R Publishing, LLC)
Paloma Books
PO Box 3531
Ashland, OR 97520
email: sales@palomabooks.com

Interior & Cover Design: L. Redding

ISBN: 978-1-55571-988-3

Printed and bound in the United States of America
First edition 10 9 8 7 6 5 4 3 2 1

The Sea Gulls Are Calling

A Mystery on the High Seas

MABEL WREN

Paloma Books   BOOKS   Ashland, Oregon

Dedicated to
the Sandy Hook Pilots

Contents

~1~

Surprises

"OH! I'M SO SCARED," wailed Lexie. She had one hand held over her upset stomach and the other hand over her forehead as if to hold her brain in place. "What if we don't like it there?"

"We will, stupid," answered her brother Bill. "Anyway we have to."

Their suitcases, which they'd just put down for a brief rest, hampered them. Only yesterday they'd left London, the city they'd lived in for their entire lives, twelve years for Lexie, fourteen for Bill, and together with their parents had taken a train to Southampton on the south coast of England. After spending the night in a hotel they had breakfast, did some last-minute shopping, and ate lunch. Then their father called a taxi to take them to the dock for passenger ships.

Now they could see the *Ocean Queen* that would take them across the Atlantic. It was so much larger than any ships they'd seen going up and down the River Thames. In only five days they would cross the Atlantic Ocean and arrive in America not for a vacation but, as far as Lexie knew, forever. That thought slowed her down.

"Come on scaredy cat, scaredy cat, scaredy cat," chanted Bill as he picked up his suitcase once more. "We'll be on board in a minute. You'll really get scared when you see England disappearing."

Lexie focused her large, brown eyes on her brother and glared at him. "You're a great help! I don't think!" Nevertheless she picked up her suitcase and continued along the pier. "I won't be in high school there."

"Neither will I," Bill said. "We'll be in the same school though."

Pausing at the gangplank, Lexie said, "I don't think Dad should take that new job. Listen to the sea gulls calling, *Stay! Stay! Stay!*"

"You'd better get your ears checked," said Bill. "They're saying, *Go! Go! Go!*"

"Boy! You don't fool me. You do put on the big brother act," Lexie said in an annoyed tone. "When you gave Dave your cricket bat and ball last night, your knuckles showed up white. Don't try to kid me. You're worried too. You won't be captain of the cricket team there. They don't even play cricket!"

"When you get to be my age you'll find more important things to think about," Bill replied. But his progress came to a halt when he placed a foot on the gangplank. It was almost a minute before he moved his other foot off the land of his birth.

A loud bark interrupted their thoughts. It came from Buddy, their Boxer. He drew their attention to the upper end of the gangplank where their parents had just entered at the Promenade Deck high up on the side of the ship. Their father had Buddy on a leash, a suitcase, a laptop, and some papers that preoccupied him. Buddy realized the children had dropped too far behind their parents. He refused to go ahead without them. He stood firm and barked again.

"Okay! Okay! We're coming," called Lexie. "We just aren't rushing, that's all."

"Speak for yourself," said Bill, "I'd rather face what I can't avoid," and at last he began to ascend the gangplank to enter the *Ocean Queen*.

Lexie stuck her tongue out at him as she picked up her suitcase, then followed him up the gangplank. At the ship's entrance she hesitated. Biting her bottom lip she put down her suitcase once again. She looked back over the dock and land. Her eyes moistened with tears that she blinked away rapidly.

Sunlight reflecting from the water danced in patterns and threw a light show on the sides of the ships and boats in dock. The creaking of the lines holding the ship to the pier; the odor of creosote; the persistent, swooping sea gulls hoping for tidbits; and the slap, slap, slap of the water on the ship and dock distracted Lexie from her fear.

With a sigh Lexie picked up her suitcase and followed her family into the ship.

She blinked. Her misty eyes cleared. Her mouth relaxed and then dropped open in astonishment. She didn't know quite what she'd been expecting but to see signs for a beauty shop, a bank, a gym, two swimming pools, a library and a ballroom took her by surprise. People strolled around also enjoying just looking at their new surroundings.

Lexie continued to follow her parents and Bill. She was so distracted by everything around her, and so busy walking forward while looking backward, she failed to notice a man standing at the window of the jeweler's. She bumped right into him.

"Ooops! Sorry!" she apologized hastily.

"Watch where you're going," snarled the man.

He startled Lexie and she dropped her suitcase right on his foot.

"You clumsy kid!" he yelled.

Lexie grabbed her suitcase and took off as fast as she could. "Boy! What a start," she panted when she caught up with Bill. "Lucky me. I met Old Grouch."

Her father came to a halt at that moment and said, "Go down this staircase to level C. Here's the card key for cabin seven. Hang on to it. While you get settled in, I'll take Buddy to the upper deck and make arrangements with the Kennel Steward."

"Can't we have him in the cabin?" asked Lexie.

"Sorry," her father answered. "All animals have to be on the top deck."

"He's house trained," pouted Lexie. "Please, Dad. Let's take him with us."

"It's the ship's rule. Besides, he'll be much more comfortable up there. You can take your coat off when you get too warm but Buddy can't."

"Okay," Lexie said, willing to be reasonable. "See you later, Buddy, just as soon as we've checked everything is shipshape." She laughed as she patted Buddy's head then knelt down and hugged him.

"Come on! Skip this goofy goodbye stuff. Girls!" Bill said, shaking his head. "You'll see him soon. Let's find our cabin, get rid of our suitcases, and go explore."

Bill led the way down the stairs. Lexie tried to get ahead of him. They scuffled. "Alexandra! William! Stop that. At once!" Knowing from experience that neither one would willingly let the other go first, their mother added, "Both stay together or we'll just stand here and wait for your father."

Without pausing for a moment, Lexie said to Bill, "Watch out. Our full names were used." They matched each other carefully foot by foot down the stairs.

"Stop!" called Mother. Lexie and Bill, so engrossed in keeping exactly with each other, were heading down towards D level.

"I knew we'd arrived," said Bill. "I just wanted to see if my dumb sister noticed."

"Oh! Just like you're so smart," answered Lexie, sticking her tongue out at Bill.

"Stop that. Right now!" said their mother. "I think I'll see the Captain about changing the ship's rules. The journey would be pleasanter if Buddy travels in the cabin and you go in the kennels. Buddy is house trained."

"Well! How'd you like that?" Bill asked.

Nobody bothered to answer him because they'd reached cabin #7.

As soon as Mother opened the door they went in. Lexie's eyebrows lifted as she had another surprise that day. "Wow! This is smashing! We have our own balcony." She opened the drapes completely on the sliding glass door as she spoke.

There were two single beds and a double, a closet, one large chest of drawers, and two tables. "Leave that smaller table for Dad's laptop," said Mother.

Bill rushed over to a door that had been left open. "Here's the bathroom."

Mother said, "We've just enough room in the drawers for what is in our suitcases. Do you see why everything else had to be sent ahead as storage?"

"Sure do," answered Bill. "Well, I'll sleep here, but only when I must. I'll take an interest in everything except sleep. I'm not going to miss a thing."

"There just might be something you'd rather miss," said Lexie, "especially if you cross paths with the old grouch I just met."

Mother gave a wide yawn. "Getting up at four a.m. yesterday and six a.m. today definitely is not my cup of tea! I'm walking in my sleep. It's close to dinnertime. I'll try to stay awake. Let's wash off the day's dirt and be ready to eat when Dad gets here."

Lexie got to the mirror first. Bill pushed her away from it impatiently as she started to experiment with her long, blonde hair. It refused to curl at the bottom after a morning in the moist sea air.

"Girls!" Bill said with disgust.

"Boys!" Lexie sneered as he plastered water on his fair hair and flattened it as straight as he could. Lexie couldn't resist poking her tongue out at him again. A new verbal battle was prevented by the arrival of their father.

"Buddy's not very happy about being far away from us but he'll have to get used to it," he reported. " This is very pleasant," he said as he looked around their cabin. "We should be very comfortable here. Now as soon as I can get a turn to wash my hands we can try out the food I've heard so much about. I'm hungry. Then we'll begin our five days of no worries and nothing to do but relax, then relax again, and then relax some more as we inhale healthy ocean breezes away from all air pollution. How wonderful."

Mother yawned. "I've lost so much sleep with all the work involved in selling our house and furniture, and deciding what to keep and pack and what must go. It is hard to let go of some things. Let's go straight to bed after dinner so that we can get up refreshed tomorrow and start our five-day vacation between jobs."

"Yes. I could look forward to an early night," said Father. "I'm exhausted. We don't know what we might have to cope with in our new life, but if we're well rested we'll be up to the challenge."

"Just like grown-ups. They're so boring. Why would any normal person want more sleep on their first cruise?" whispered Lexie to Bill as they all left the cabin.

They went back to the main staircase, carefully finding their way between the many passengers as new to this ship as themselves.

"I wonder how many people are on this ship," Lexie said, as she threaded her way among them with care so as to avoid bumping into anybody else.

Father answered, "According to the pamphlet I picked up at the office, three thousand passengers are able to sleep in the cabins."

Mother added, "I've read it takes over a thousand workers or more to run this ship. It goes from England to the USA in five days. It's a floating vacation resort."

By this time they had arrived at the restaurant. Father pushed open the glass doors for them. They were greeted by a friendly host and soon seated at a table.

A table steward approached. "Hello," he said. "I'm Tom. Welcome aboard."

"Hello Tom, I'm Joe Costa. Meet my wife Cathy, and our children, Lexie and Bill."

"I hope you'll have a wonderful trip," replied Tom, as he quickly handed out the menus. "This is an English ship but we serve favorite foods from many countries."

"Oh Boy!" Bill exclaimed when he saw the choices. "I'd like something of everything. Is this how we're going to eat in the New World?"

"Several cooks and a table steward are only for the next five days Bill. Then it's life as usual," his mother pointed out. "You'll get back to earth in more ways than one."

At that moment Lexie saw the man she'd already named Old Grouch enter by the glass doors. The host greeted him and then started to walk with him towards the table where the Costa's were seated. Several more people could be seated with them.

"Oh no!" Lexie whispered to Bill. "Look who's coming this way." She bent her head over the table hoping her hair would hide her face. Then her shoulders relaxed as they walked right past her. She looked up to see the host had seated Old Grouch at a table a comfortable distance away.

Suddenly she heard her father say, "Didn't you hear me Lexie?"

"What?" she asked.

"Your order. Tom has many other passengers to serve."

"Oh! Sorry. Let me see."

Then, although Lexie appeared to be giving her full attention to the menu selection, she really focused on the man who'd been so rude to her. Something about him puzzled her. She couldn't put her finger on just why he made her feel uneasy. She'd noticed his grim mouth. He looked so ordinary she thought. He wore light tan trousers and matching jacket over a green and white checkered shirt. He had a slight limp and used a walking stick. His eyebrows seemed etched in a permanent frown. His eyes! Yes. That's it. She remembered now. He didn't look straight at her even when shouting at her. His eyes were constantly on the move. Searching? Avoiding? Watching?

~2~

New Friends
and Mystery

N EXT MORNING WHEN LEXIE woke up she thought
her mother and father were still asleep. She'd left
her tennis shoes, green jeans, and a hummingbird decorated T-shirt handy the night before, hoping to be first to
the bathroom. When she'd dressed, Lexie tiptoed over to
Bill's bed where he lay with the covers over his face. She
jabbed where she thought his ribs might be.

Immediately his head appeared over the covers. "Stop
it! I wasn't snoring."

"Shh! Don't wake up Mum and Dad. Let's go exploring
and see Buddy."

"Okay. Let's eat first, though." As he headed for the
bathroom he added, " I'm starving."

Lexie looked at his slim body with envy. "Okay" she

agreed, "but there are more important things to do than eat."

"Maybe," he agreed, "but I like to start with eating." He disappeared into the bathroom and soon reappeared in blue jeans, black tennis shoes, and a "Save the Planet" T-shirt.

"Let's go," Lexie whispered."

"Where are you going this early in the morning?" asked Father with a yawn as he opened his eyes. Looking at his watch he added, "It's only seven a.m."

"We're just going to look around," answered Lexie.

"Well don't make any noise. It's two hours 'til the tide's in and that's when the Captain will sound the warning whistle to all boats and ships around to get out of the shipping lane. We'll be leaving immediately. I want you back in this cabin before that to eat some gingersnaps to prevent travel sickness."

"I'd better give some to Buddy too. I don't want him to get sick," said Lexie. She reached inside the package on top of the suitcases for a handful. "See you later."

Bill reached for two hands of gingersnaps. Then he and Lexie left quietly. They didn't talk until they reached the staircase.

As they arrived at the shopping center Lexie said, "Look, we can get our photos printed here. See that sign on the jeweler's window. It's hard to believe we're on a ship."

Bill said, " It looks as if you can get almost anything done. You can go to the Beauty Shop to get your hair curled instead of taking up time in the bathroom for hours. They must have been expecting you."

They'd reached the restaurant. "Say, look at this." Bill

pointed to some writing on the door. "I missed this last night. Breakfast is served from seven to nine a.m. Lunch from noon 'til two p.m. Dinner from six-thirty to eight-thirty p.m. If we come for a meal as soon as the restaurant opens we can eat breakfast for two hours. Then we can come for a two-hour lunch at noon. Followed by a two-hour dinner at six-thirty p.m. I'm really going to enjoy this trip. We could eat for a lot longer by ordering a big dish fifteen minutes before closing time and that might take another hour to eat."

"I don't think so," replied Lexie, "but you won't starve. See what it says here. Snacks are served in all lounges throughout the day and night. They must have been expecting you, Bill."

Bill pushed open the door, held it back for Lexie and tipped an imaginary hat to her so dramatically that Lexie wished there were steps she could trip him down as she thanked him ever so politely.

They knew their table. As they sat down, Tom came over and handed them the menu and a schedule of the activities on board for that day.

"Good morning," Tom said. "What would you like for your hot dish?"

Bill answered promptly, "Anything you can fry together will do for me. Potatoes, eggs, bread, tomatoes, bacon, mushrooms, sausages—would be a good start."

"I'll have bacon, two scrambled eggs, and some toast please," Lexie answered.

"Jolly good. While this is cooking," said Tom, "help yourself to fruit or juice and cold cereal from the buffet. It's not good to travel on an empty stomach." He winked at Lexie as he said this, then looked at Bill. He left to give their orders to the cook.

As Lexie and Bill began their cereal and milk, two other children came over and sat down at their table.

"Hi! I'm Glen," said the boy, who was close to Bill's age but not quite as tall. Glen's hair and eyes were dark brown.

"Hello! I'm Bill and this is my sister, Lexie."

"Hi! I'm Debby," said the girl. She was about Lexie's age, slim and with rich auburn hair. She added, "I heard you talking to the steward. You two do have a strong accent. Where are you from?"

"We're from London but you're the ones with accents," said Lexie. "You should hear yourselves. Where are you from?"

Debby answered, "California." Then she added, "Californians don't have accents. We speak normally."

Lexie and Bill burst out laughing. Bill mimicked, emphasizing the drawled "a" sound, "Caaaalifornians have no accent." He shook with laughter. "You are very funny."

At that moment Tom returned with the hot food. He also gave them a pot of tea, butter, and marmalade. He placed a rack holding six pieces of toast near Bill. "Will that be enough toast?" he inquired.

"For me, yes," said Bill. "But my sister wants some."

"One slice will be enough for me. Do you think you can manage with five? I'm not going to sit here all day and watch you eat," said Lexie.

"I'll rough it if that's how you feel little sister," replied Bill with a phony sigh.

Then Tom addressed Debby and Glen. "Hi! Orange juice and cereal are at the buffet. Help yourself. What would you like for a hot dish?"

Debby said, "I'll have milk, hot cakes with syrup, and one egg over easy."

Glen added, "The same for me except make that two eggs, please."

Now Lexie and Bill looked puzzled.

"Why do you eat cake for breakfast?" asked Bill.

"And why eat cake hot? We wait for it to cool," added Lexie.

Tom explained, "Hot cakes are small pancakes. Eggs over easy are turned over for a short time but the yolk is still runny when served. I'm English but I have to learn both languages on this job. I expect Debby thinks a bonnet is something to wear on her head. You'd have to explain to her it covers the engine of a car." Tom left.

Debby said, "We've learned some English on our two-week vacation. It took us a while to know that...'I have to spend a penny' means I have to go to the toilet! Our toilets are usually a quarter."

"A quarter of what?" asked Lexie.

"A dollar of course," explained Bill.

Lexie frowned. "I didn't think we'd have any trouble with the language. I thought Americans spoke English!"

Tom had just returned and he heard Lexie's last remark. "Well, you're in for some surprises," he commented as he handed out food. "You'll have to relearn some of your spelling too. Most puzzling of all are the words that sound the same but they have a different meaning on each side of the Atlantic."

"It sounds very confusing," commented Bill.

"It is," replied Tom. "You'll soon get used to a strange look coming on someone's face as you're talking. Then you'll know it's time to ask questions and try to clean up the mess you just talked yourself into. Good luck!" He left to attend to the next table.

"Let's eat," said Glen. "After two weeks of foreign food I'm ready to taste an American breakfast again."

Lexie checked the program (provided daily at each table) for activities on board ship. "Crummy! Swimming all daylight hours," said Lexie, with her mouth full.

"What's crummy about swimming?" asked Debby. "I like to swim."

"So do I," said Lexie.

"Then why did you say crummy swimming?" asked Debby. Lexie looked puzzled.

Bill laughed. "You both have that look on your face that Tom just talked about." They looked at him with their eyebrows raised.

"You're both speaking different languages but saying the same words. Get it?" Lexie, Debby and Glen shook their heads "no."

"Crummy doesn't mean anything in English. It is just an exclamation of surprise. In America it means no good. Isn't that right, Glen?"

"Yes."

"Oh! Crummy!" giggled Lexie. "I think I'd better change the subject. Debby would you like to meet our dog, Buddy? He's a Boxer. We'll be spending as much time as possible with him on the top deck where the kennels are. Why don't you come up there when you're through eating?"

"I love animals. Sure, I'd like to meet Buddy."

"So would I," added Glen. "It will have to be later because we have to go back to our cabin. Our parents are expecting us. We'll take a rain check on the invitation."

Bill pushed back his chair while wiping his mouth on his hand. He spoke to Lexie, "Are you ready? I've earned money by mowing lawns. Now I can get a watch. I've already talked with Dad about the one I want. I'll see if they have it at the jeweler's. I must be on time for meals. "

Lexie already had her food scraps, rather large ones wrapped in a napkin, but Mother wasn't around, She went to get Bill's leftovers then shrugged her shoulders and gave a sigh when she found he'd left nothing for Buddy.

Lexie and Bill made their way to the Upper Deck reserved for animals. They spotted Buddy before he saw them. He looked utterly miserable lying down with his head sunk on his forepaws. His eyes stared straight ahead. A dish of food and a bowl of water lay untouched beside him. Suddenly he raised his head, with his ears erect.

"Buddy! Buddy!" yelled Lexie.

Buddy changed in an instant. He jumped, barked, and wagged his tail all at the same time. Lexie took Buddy out of the kennel and put him on a leash. Then Lexie stroked his back and shook his paw. Buddy especially liked to shake hands if he had done something wrong. He needed to be reassured that everything was all right again after a reprimand. Buddy held his paw up again and again and barked excitedly.

"It's all right, Buddy." Lexie tried to calm him. "You haven't done anything wrong. I wish I could make you understand what is going on. You'll only have to be here for a few days, and we'll visit with you every day."

Bill added, "You could be with us when we get to America. New breeding lines of purebred dogs are wanted there. That's what finally persuaded Mum and Dad to bring you. Not that they wanted to leave you with anyone. You're family."

"I would never have left without you," said Lexie as she held a gingersnap up high. Buddy liked this trick. He stood on his back legs and turned and turned and turned until Lexie dropped the treat right into his waiting mouth. "Do you want another one?" asked Lexie. "Well, ask for it then. I don't want to force you to eat gingersnaps."

Low rumbles came from Buddy's throat.

"Can you say that a bit louder?" asked Lexie. Louder noises, almost a bark, came from Buddy. "Not quite that loud, Buddy!"

Quieter noises came from Buddy.

"That's better," said Lexie tossing the gingersnap to Buddy. "Eat that up so you don't get sick when we get going up and down on the ocean waves." Then Lexie fed her Boxer egg, bacon, and buttered toast scraps.

Bill said, "I'll close the gate then we can play ball with Buddy." He started toward the gate but a sudden commotion from the bottom of the short flight of steps that led up to the Upper Deck made them both stop what they were doing to listen.

They heard a man with a deep voice say, "How are we going to get these dogs settled on board? Do you want to go up the steps first and have me get the dogs up to you one at a time?"

A woman's voice answered, "No! I don't WANT to. These steps are ridiculous. I thought we were going to be on a passenger ship not a cargo boat."

The man answered, "I've been trying to get it across to you that you'd be able to get around better if you'd change out of those high heels and wear sandals. Anyway, one of us has to go up first. Who's it to be?"

"I s'pose I'd better go first," said the woman. Then she almost screamed, "I can't get up these steps. They're far too steep!"

"I told you to wear flats and pants while on board. You wouldn't listen. Now you have a choice. Take off your high heels or your skirt, which ever is easier."

Lexie and Bill ducked as a high-heeled shoe came whizzing by them. They waited, alert. Then came the second shoe thrown so high Lexie thought it would go overboard. Then a curly blonde head appeared followed by a slim attractive body. The woman smoothed her skirt and patted her hair in place. Eventually she called to the man, "One at a time."

Lexie counted as five, white, beautifully groomed miniature poodles came up the steps onto the animal deck followed by one Toy poodle with the same hair style trim as the other five.

"Oo--oo-oo," Lexie murmured. "They are so cute."

The blonde didn't seem to agree with her, although Buddy whimpered his appreciation.

The woman only became more nervous. "Patti, Matti, Hatti—stop that. Fifi, Gigi, Migi—stop too. George! George!" she squealed. "Come and get these dogs. AT ONCE! Do you hear me?"

Her voice only made the dogs more active. "Shut up you awful creatures," she yelled. They ran around and around her, tying her legs together with their leashes. Then they all pulled in one direction and the woman gave a scream as she hit the deck.

Lexie and Bill rushed over to help her. Lexie asked, "Are you hurt?"

"Yes I'm hurt," the woman replied fretfully, "but nothing is broken. Oh! I never should have come on this trip! Five whole days and nights just wasted on the Atlantic Ocean. I want something more interesting to look at than water, water, and more water. How utterly boring! I told George I didn't want to handle these dogs. Shut up you awful creatures!" she yelled again.

"I'm coming dear," called a man. The voice added, "Up boy."

Lexie's eyes opened wide as the biggest dog she'd ever seen appeared. "Crummy!" she exclaimed. "Bill have you ever seen a dog that big before?"

"Lexie, don't you know anything? He's a Great Dane."

"I know WHAT he is but I never knew they were THAT big. He is spectacular"

Another "Up boy!" and a sleek, dark German Shepherd bounded onto the deck followed by George, mopping his brow with a large handkerchief.

Seeing that his dogs were exchanging inquisitive sniffs with Buddy and wagging their tails, he attended to his unhappy wife. Lexie and Bill retrieved the high-heeled shoes and took them back to their owner.

While still sitting on the deck tied up with leashes, George's wife continued to gripe about her fate. She whined, "As if it's not bad enough entering those dogs in shows all over the British Isles, now we have to go all the way to America. I wouldn't mind if we could go to Hollywood. Maybe I could become a movie star. I'm very photogenic." She preened her hair. "But No! No! Only the dogs matter to George."

George appeared to ignore the tirade. He patiently unwound each leash. Then Lexie and Bill took turns putting each dog in a kennel. When the last one had been locked in George helped his wife stand. Then he patted Buddy's head. Buddy licked his hand and wagged his tail.

Now that the woman seemed calm Lexie decided to risk saying something that had been on her mind for the past few minutes. "You're so lucky to have eight dogs. Our parents will only let us have one."

"I don't see anything lucky about owning eight dogs, but if you like dogs that much maybe you can help my husband with them. He's arranged to give a show on board this ship. Just to keep the dogs in practice he says, but I know better don't I George? You'll take any chance you get to show off those dogs! Anyway, can these kids help you with the show?"

"If they'd like to," George said, mopping his brow.

"I'd LOVE to!" Lexie replied eagerly.

"So would I," said Bill.

"Okay. My show is scheduled for the second night at sea. What are your names?" He listened then said, "Well, just call me George. Meet my wife, Mrs. Bryant. Now my dear why don't we get you that pair of earrings you admired in the jeweler's window."

As they prepared to leave that deck Lexie said, "I can't wait for the show! Buddy's got plenty of company now. By the way his ears perked up when the six cute poodles arrived and stopped by to say hello makes me wonder if he'll miss us at all."

"We'd better get going," Bill said, and took Buddy to his kennel.

"Just a minute." Lexie pointed to another dog that they

hadn't noticed before. With all the barking from nine other dogs this one hadn't moved or made a noise. "Can we do anything to cheer him or her up?" Lexie asked.

"No. We can't but his owner can. Buddy looked glum before he saw us." Lexie walked quietly to the dog, a St. Bernard. "Come here. I've got a treat for you." A low rumble came from the dog's throat. She knelt on the deck and flipped her last piece of toast to him.

The St. Bernard sniffed at the scrap then looked at Lexie. Another rumble came from the dog's throat. Lexie wasn't sure if the noise was friendly or not.

Suddenly a voice yelled, "What are you doing there? Get away from that dog!" All the dogs except the St. Bernard began to bark.

Lexie jumped up and backed away. It came as no surprise to her to find that the owner of the gruff voice was the man she'd bumped into the previous evening. She felt her cheeks getting hot. This time she decided she would not apologize. She didn't think she'd done anything wrong. As the man approached she noticed something odd. She asked, "Is that your dog?"

"Yes." the gruff voice answered. "Stay away from him! Don't go anywhere near him. Certainly not! Definitely not! Absolutely not! Do you hear me?" He raised his walking stick and shook it at her in a threatening manner as he said this. "When I find a kennel steward I'll tell him about you interfering with my dog. Now scram!"

"We were just leaving," said Bill as he walked towards the steps to a lower deck. Lexie followed him so closely she almost tripped.

When they got down to the next deck, Lexie turned to

Bill and said, "Did you notice anything suspicious?"

"No! I did not! Please don't go using your vivid imagination."

"It's not my imagination," she answered excitedly. "Didn't you notice that when Old Grouch arrived the St. Bernard didn't wag its tail or seem in any way pleased to see him. Now that is odd. That's why I asked Old Grouch if he owned the dog. Buddy was so happy to see us. Why didn't the St. Bernard perk up? Buddy barked but didn't wag his tail when Old Grouch turned up. Buddy's usually friendly with everyone. I don't think he likes Old Grouch. I wonder why?"

~3~

Lexie Challenges Bill

BILL SAID, "WE'D BETTER hurry. I'll race you back to the cabin if you promise not to bump into any more suspicious strangers. You're making me bite my fingernails with worry."

"Okay, smarty. You just may be biting your nails with worry before this trip is over. Anyway, I'm not going to race. I've got to keep my eyes open and stay alert. I don't want to miss anything. I could use a map to find my way around this ship though, it's so huge. Hey! Where are all the people?"

"I expect they're all up on deck waiting for the big moment of leaving the pier." They were descending the main staircase and arrived in the corridor to their cabin to see their parents standing outside the cabin door carrying cameras.

"We thought you'd never get here," Mother said impatiently. She handed them their cameras. "Dad said you took enough gingersnaps to prevent the entire British Navy getting seasick, so I presume you don't need more."

As they hurried up the stairs, Father said, "You'll be able to write to your English friends about interesting things that they aren't likely to experience. "

"I'm sure of that," said Lexie with a glance at Bill.

They came out onto the main deck just in time. Sailors were hauling in the lines. A long blast on the ship's whistle and then they were moving. People on the quay started to wave goodbye and the passengers crowded at the railings waved back. Lexie's stomach did flip-flops. She'd been so concerned about Old Grouch and the dog he claimed to be his, she'd forgotten that she was leaving all that was familiar. After they left the dock she saw one-family brick houses, and other ships, boats, and cranes of many different sizes. She noticed her father squeeze her mother's hand and put his arms around her. They didn't talk though. Lexie didn't feel like talking either.

Bill called, "Come on. Let's get some photos. I want to see how many tugs are taking us out of the harbor."

"I don't think I will," said Lexie. "I'm getting seasick."

"Oh! Don't be stupid!" said Bill. "You can't be getting seasick. We're not out at sea yet. This is still the harbor. Come on! There's lots to see in a harbor."

Lexie thought she might feel better if she didn't watch the land they were leaving behind. "Okay. I'm on my way," she replied.

Father called loudly, "Watch for the Isle of Wight. If you're in the right place you might see the pilot leave this ship and get into his own boat to return to the dock."

"What's a pilot doing on a ship?" asked Lexie. " I thought pilots flew planes."

"Oh boy! Don't girls know anything?" asked Bill.

"That's just one kind of pilot. Ships need pilots who know the local waters to guide them in and out of harbors. The Captain doesn't take over until out at sea."

"I'm glad I asked," Lexie said. "I forgot you're a walking encyclopedia." Although she answered breezily she really felt put down all the time by Bill. She admitted to herself that he really knew a lot and he excelled at sports. She hid her hurt feeling as usual and opened her camera to be ready to snap some scenes.

As they went down another set of steps to a lower deck Lexie's seasick feeling disappeared. "Look!" she exclaimed. "There's Old Grouch in a deck chair reading a newspaper. Let's stick around for a while and watch him."

Bill answered, " We'll be on this ship with him for five days. You can watch him later. I want to get photos of the pilot, his boat, the tugs, and the navigation tower at the end of the harbor and I only have a few minutes."

"There's one tug. While you get a picture of it I'll keep an eye on Old Grouch. Hey! Just a minute. He's smiling as he reads. What on earth could make him smile? Don't get in my way. I want a picture of that. I got it. Whew! That must be a once in a lifetime event."

"Let's go and find the other tugs," said Bill as if Lexie hadn't spoken.

"Okay. No. Wait. Old Grouch is leaving."

Old Grouch got up, dropped the newspaper on the deck chair and walked off still chuckling. Lexie dashed over and picked up the newspaper.

Bill walked over and said impatiently, "Come on. What's so odd about someone reading a newspaper and smiling? Maybe he was reading the comics."

"Not on the front page," she said as she quickly scanned the headlines. "There's a strike...two cars and a bus in an accident. . .Today in Parliament...I don't see anything funny." She read quietly a few more moments. Then she exclaimed, "Listen to this: *Jewel Robbery. Actress Renee Glamoure, reported the the theft of a priceless jewel collection. She discovered her loss on her return from the USA. The police have no clues. The voyage of Miss Glamoure was kept secret. A generous reward is being offered for the return of the jewels or for information that leads to the arrest of the thief or thieves.* Old Grouch wasn't just smiling, he was gloating!

"You've got to admit there's something strange about that man. Every time I see him something unusual happens. I'm getting more and more curious."

"You're impossible," said Bill. "Just because you solved the lunchbox mystery of the disappearing crisps, I suppose now you want to go to the Captain and report that you saw a man smiling as he read the newspaper. He acted like any human and didn't like you dropping your suitcase on his foot and he grumbled at you. You gave his dog table scraps without his permission.

"Take your big brother's advice: avoid that man for the rest of the journey. Gosh! Listening to your nonsense I've nearly missed the photos I want. Look! There's the Isle of Wight. The tugs have almost finished their job. They'll head back to the pier soon."

Bill dashed off. Lexie followed. She wanted some pictures too. She knew she would have to find some facts before Bill would listen to her intuition. She'd have to go over the events and talk with Bill later. They ran from bow to stern clicking their cameras frequently. While Lexie took photos of the graceful sea gulls following the ship, hoping for scraps of food, Bill watched for the navigation tower.

"I can see it," Bill said. "Lexie come here NOW! The pilot will be leaving any moment."

Lexie hurried over to the railing and joined him just in time to see the pilot descend some rope steps on the side of the *Ocean Queen*. The steps ended quite a few feet above the water. The pilot jumped from the last rung and landed upright in his own boat.

"I hope that picture comes out," said Lexie. "I think I caught him in mid-air just above his boat."

"I did too. I'd like to see that dog trainer's wife do that," laughed Bill.

"I'd like to see you do it. I wonder how many times the pilot went into the water when he began his job," added Lexie. A sudden lurch of the ship sent her grabbing for a railing and holding tight.

The pilot 's boat and the four tugs turned and headed back toward the dock.

The *Ocean Queen*, now in the English Channel between England and France, headed west toward the Atlantic. Now the Captain was in charge of the great ship and her passengers.

"Wow!" said Lexie. "I can feel the movement now. It's quite gentle but not like walking on land." They were definitely leaving land behind. The sky was gray. A slight drizzle moistened her cheeks. The weather matched her mood. She wondered what l lay ahead in her cruise and a new land.

Her gloomy feeling disappeared slightly and she laughed at the sight of the sea gulls swooping for food scraps that suddenly came from a porthole. She wondered if this was the restaurant area and if this explained why the sea gulls followed the ship as if drawn by a magnet. A sudden larger swell made her cling to the railing for a moment. "Won't it be strange, Bill, to see only water for days and days and days and days?"

"Well it will be different, that's for sure," said Bill. "I think I'm getting my sea legs. It's fun. But wait until we get out in the middle of the Atlantic. Huge waves will come crashing over the deck." Seeing a worried frown appear on Lexie's face Bill added, "Everything not lashed down will be swept overboard, including men, women, and children. Only half the passengers ever reach the other shore."

A message over the ship's intercom prevented Lexie's response.

"This is your Captain speaking. Welcome aboard the *Ocean Queen*. As a safety precaution we will soon have a lifeboat drill."

"What did I tell you?" whispered Bill.

The Captain continued, "Don't let this worry you. This ship has crossed the Atlantic hundreds of times without a mishap other than a few broken dishes."

Lexie glared at Bill. "I'll believe the Captain but not your story. He knows what he is talking about."

"In case of an emergency," continued the Captain, "you must know how to leave the ship in a safe manner and without panic. Please return to your cabins now and read the instructions on the door. It will tell you where you report to your lifeboat station. Get your life jackets out of the cupboard and put them on as shown in the picture on the front. When you hear the warning siren, go quickly but without running, and assemble at your lifeboat station. There, a steward will check if your jacket is on correctly and check your name on his roll call. A second siren indicates the practice is over. *Bon Voyage!*"

As Lexie and Bill returned to their cabin Lexie said to Bill, "You don't know much about modern travel do you? Your information is centuries out of date. You must have read too many books about the *Mayflower*, the *Niña*, the *Santa Maria*, and the *Pinta*."

"I just like to tease my little sister."

"I'd like to trip you down the stairs if there weren't so many people around. Wait! I'm not going below yet. This would be a good time to follow Old Grouch to his cabin." She stopped by the jeweler's and pretended to be looking at the rings in the window.

"Why don't you leave that man alone?" asked Bill, a warning note in his voice. Lexie disregarded him. She saw Debby and Glen approaching with their parents.

She waved to them. They waved back, then walked over to Bill and Lexie.

Debby said, "If we find we have to be at the same lifeboat station as you, Bill, you'd better cut down on your eating. We'll sink if you always eat as much as you did this morning."

Lexie said, "I've tried to get him to quit stuffing himself but it's a losing battle. It would be easier to throw him overboard, Debby."

"Man overboard is serious business," said Glen. "Bill, I'll keep my sister in line if you can handle yours."

He took Debby firmly around the shoulders and guided her below.

Lexie felt relief that they'd left because at that moment she saw Old Grouch. "Pretend to look in the window," she said to Bill. "You know who is coming. I'm going to follow him. You do as you like."

"I certainly will," answered Bill. "I'll follow him. I've wondered if his limp is real."

When Old Grouch passed by they followed him cautiously. He turned off the main staircase at B level. Other people did too so they had no difficulty in following him unnoticed. He entered a cabin without using a key. They observed the number "22" on the door.

Lexie asked Bill, "Wouldn't you think he'd lock his cabin?"

Bill commented, "Well, I'd assume he hasn't got the Crown Jewels in there."

"I'm just looking for clues right now," answered Lexie. "We'd better hurry back to our cabin and get our life jackets."

Once again their parents, already in their life jackets, were waiting for them. A siren sounded. A mournful noise.

"Slip these on," said Mother. "Then we go to the Promenade Deck where we'll see lifeboat number ten."

As they made their way to the promenade deck Lexie told her parents "We've been invited to help a man with his dog show on board ship."

"Well, I don't like the thought of you handling other peoples' dogs, especially at sea. All the motion is bound to make the dogs extra nervous."

"We can do it, Mum. Oops! I mean, Mom! I'd better speak American," said Bill.

Father said, "Lexie does have a way with animals. I think she could handle anything however nervous it became. Bill would be O.K. too."

Mother said, "First I'll inquire if an adult will be around at all times, and if all the animals have had the proper immunizations. If so, it will be all right."

"Oh Mum, thanks," said Lexie, "they're beautiful animals and I'm sure George takes proper care of them. He's so proud of them. His wife doesn't share his enthusiasm. She's the one who suggested we help him."

"I'm glad to hear there are other dogs on board now. That will help Buddy. How was he this morning?" asked Father.

"Once he saw us he perked up in a hurry," Lexie answered.

They approached a group of people gathered around lifeboat number ten. Lexie commented, "Look at all the other groups at intervals along the deck."

A steward came toward them. He held a clipboard and pen. "Your names?" Father answered for them.

The steward checked them off his list. Then he inspected their life jackets. "Good." Now everybody is here." He addressed the group. "I'm Jack Harris your Deck Steward and in charge of this lifeboat. It's equipped with food, first aid needs, rope, and a whistle in case of fog. If there should be an emergency dress warmly and comfortably. Put on your life jackets. Bring any personal essential medicine. There's plenty of general medicine in the emergency kit. Come here immediately. Your life and the lives of others depend on your quick response. We do have five passengers who are deaf and one who is blind. They've been given private instructions. If anyone has any health problem that needs special consideration speak to me about your needs now. Well, that's it. If you'd like to get acquainted with other passengers, go ahead. If you have any questions I'm here to answer them."

The wailing siren, indicating the lifeboat drill was over, prevented talk. When the noise stopped, Debby and Glen came over.

Debby asked, "Why don't we go swimming together every day? Now we know Bill will be in our lifeboat we have a definite need to see that he exercises."

"That sounds like a good idea," said Bill.

"Oh!" said Lexie. "I didn't know you thought a girl could have a good idea, Bill." Bill's cheeks colored a little but he wasn't lost for words.

"Sisters are different!" He took off at a run.

"Why don't we go to lunch?" laughed Glen. "On the way, Lexie, I could give you some tips on how to keep a brother in his place. I should know. I have three older sisters and they got in a lot of practice on me."

They walked along together chatting pleasantly. By the time they got to the restaurant, Bill had been served already. He looked up but didn't stop eating. By the time the others had given their lunch requests to Tom, Bill gave his order for dessert—apple pie and three scoops of ice cream. "This sea air is making me ravenous," Bill said. "I'll rest in a deck chair before we go for that swim. Hurry up you three. You ARE slow. There's more to life than eating."

"Wow!" said Debby. "Lexie, I think you've really let your brother get out of hand. He needs working on or you won't be able to live with him soon."

Lexie said, "We'll dunk him in the pool. I'm not very hungry. I'm not getting dessert."

Debby and Glen ordered pie and ice cream.

"While they eat let's play chess, Lexie," said Bill. He removed his traveling chess set from his pocket and placed it on the table. "I'll beat you," he stated.

"Just try," said Lexie. She smiled when she saw she could take two of Bill's pawns on her third and fourth moves.

She frowned when Bill, on his fifth move, smugly called, "Checkmate!"

Lexie felt hurt to be beaten so quickly. She'd known Bill to play a game for hours with his friend. Since no one had explained much about the game to her she didn't know she'd fallen for an old trick. She probably would have felt worse if she'd known Bill could have beaten her in fewer moves and called, "Fool's-mate."

Lexie still felt angry with Bill as they all left the restaurant for the Sports Deck. As they approached the pool, Lexie looked out across the vast Atlantic Ocean. Suddenly she turned to Bill and said, "You won with five moves in chess but I bet I can solve the mystery involving Old Grouch with five moves!"

"Who or what is Old Grouch? Debby asked. "A new deck game?"

"Yes," replied Lexie. "A very new deck game! I'll tell you about it later."

Immediately she regretted making such an announcement. She wished she didn't always feel as if she were competing with Bill. What would her five moves be? She had no idea.

～4～

Magic and
Lexie's First Move

L EXIE FELT GLUM. The afternoon had been horrible.
Now she stayed pretty quiet as she had dinner with
Debby, Bill, and Glen. Bill had outshone all of them in the
pool. Far worse, although she'd thought about the problem of Old Grouch most of the time she hadn't any idea
of even her first move. She didn't want to let her new
friends in on her hunch until she had something a little
more definite to tell them. Bill already thought of her as
stupid; she didn't want Debby and Glen to agree with him.

The ship's movement in a bigger wave interrupted her
thoughts. Dishes went sliding across the table. They'd almost finished dinner so there was little liquid to spill.
Built up rims around the table prevented dishes breaking
on the floor and food falling into their laps. As they re-

placed the dishes in front of themselves and everything settled down again Lexie inquired, "Who'd like to go to the magic show?"

"That's little kids' stuff," answered Bill.

"No it isn't," said Debby. "This guy is great. I've seen him on TV. It would be a terrific way to spend an evening."

"We can sit near a door then, if we don't like it, we could slip out easily," said Bill.

"Let's give it a try," suggested Glen. "We can see if we can figure out the tricks ourselves. That might be even more fun."

They helped themselves to a handful of sugar cubes and wandered down to the lounge. Lexie watched the sunset through a porthole. "It's beautiful," she said. "Come and look." She walked from porthole to porthole. Lexie suddenly gave a gasp. She'd been enjoying the gold-edged clouds so much she hadn't noticed Old Grouch. He sat reading at a small table near the next porthole. She quickly recovered from the shock. Then she decided to walk right past him and see what magazine he held in his hand that had him so engrossed. Bill continued to follow her.

When they got past Old Grouch Bill said, in a mysterious voice, "Don't you think there's something odd about a man with a dog who reads a dog magazine?"

Lexie glared at Bill. Debby and Glen exchanged puzzled looks. Debby asked, "Are you speaking English again and there's something we don't understand?"

Lexie shook her head "no." Then she held her finger to her lips and pointed toward the door with her other hand. The Purser had entered followed by a small man in a long, multicolored cape, a tall gray hat, and a sparkling white shirt with a red cravat. They carried boxes and put them down on some tables that had been set up earlier.

Old Grouch made a mark in the magazine. He looked up and saw the lounge had filled up with many adults and children in rows of seats.

The Purser held up his hand for silence. "We're very lucky to have Melvin the Magician on board. He's worried his magic might disappear by the time he gets to New York if he doesn't keep in practice, so he's offered to put on a show."

Melvin bowed low with a flourish of his hat. He received a round of applause. This disturbed Old Grouch in his reading. He looked around. "What are all these kids doing here?" he muttered. "Why don't the parents keep their little darlings in their own cabins?" He hunched his shoulders and concentrated on his magazine.

Melvin announced, "I would like a helper."

Lexie jumped to her feet at once. "O-oo-oo pick me. Please," she said. Many other hands raised. "Please! Please!" said Lexie.

"Since you're so keen young lady, I'll have you." He held out his hand to her. "Your name is...?" He introduced Lexie to the audience. "I'm glad to have you as my assistant but please don't run off with my props," he said, casually removing three ping pong balls from her nose. Lexie giggled.

"In case you get too troublesome," Melvin said, "I'd better see if I can take away your strength. See if you can pick up this box from the table."

Lexie picked up the box without effort. Melvin took it from her and placed the box back on the table. "Just as I expected," Melvin announced to the audience. "This young lady could carry off everything I own. Look at this. " He removed a large, gold circle from each of Lexie's ears. She looked puzzled.

"Now I'll put a stop to that," the magician said as he grasped her arms where they met her shoulders and then acted as if he were squeezing something out of them, moving his hands firmly and slowly down to her fingertips. He shook his hands as if throwing something away. "That's done it!" he said with a satisfied look on his face. "See if you can pick up that box now."

Lexie tried to pick up the box. This time she couldn't move it. She struggled with it in disbelief. She pushed. She pulled. She frowned. She tried again. It would not budge.

"If you promise not to take any more of my things I'll give you back your strength," said Melvin.

"I promise I won't take a thing," said Lexie.

This time Melvin seemed to grab something from the air, then touched Lexie's fingers and pulled something invisible up her arms to her shoulders then shook his hands over her. "Now try again," he said.

This time Lexie almost fell over because she put such an effort into lifting the box but it was light and moved easily. She laughed with relief. She didn't believe in magic. However she couldn't lift that box the second time. She was the assistant. If she'd been watching someone else do that she would assume the assistant was pretending the box had become too heavy to move. She had no further time for thought as Melvin now held up some razor blades. (This is not a trick to be tried out at home!)

"If I start to choke bang me on the back, Lexie. I'll trust you to save my life." Melvin appeared to swallow six razor blades as the audience counted them. Then he started to cough and cough.

Lexie, so engrossed in watching him, forgot she was his assistant. She knew razor blades couldn't be swallowed by anyone. She did not bang his back.

Melvin motioned to her frantically. Suddenly she remembered her job and pounded him on his back. He drew a razor blade from each ear, one from the top of his head, one from his nose and another from his mouth.

"Hit me again," he said.

Lexie gave him a loud slap on his back.

"You've done it now," he said. "It's gone for good. Be careful, Lexie. I need these things in New York."

Lexie giggled again.

"I'll risk letting you tie me up," said Melvin as he handed Lexie a rope. He sat on a straight-backed chair. Lexie tied his hands behind his back and then to the chair. She tied his ankles together and then to the chair. She stood back.

After a few wiggles and squirms Melvin stood up free of the rope.

A puzzled look crossed Lexie's face. She couldn't figure out how he did any of the tricks even though she watched him carefully.

Melvin walked over to one of his boxes on the table. "Ah, hah!" he said. "Just what I need." He removed something. "Let's see what my magic baton can do."

He walked toward Lexie. Suddenly he tripped and broke the baton. He picked up the two pieces. "Oh dear," he said. "That's a pity. I'm sorry but unless I can find another baton the show will be over."

Lexie grinned mischievously and said, "Would any stick work?"

"Well, I would try any stick," Melvin answered.

"I know where there is a nice walking stick," she volunteered. "Look there. That man has a lovely one." She pointed to Old Grouch.

Melvin walked over to the man. "Pardon me, Sir," he said. "May I borrow your cane?"

Old Grouch didn't hear. Melvin tapped him on the shoulder. "Sir, may I borrow your walking cane?"

"Certainly not!" snapped Old Grouch. "Definitely not! Absolutely not!" he added as he closed his magazine and walked away toward the door.

"Boo-oo-oo," yelled many of the children.

Old Grouch paused a moment at the EXIT sign to shake his stick at the audience in a threatening manner. Lexie noticed his walking stick was attached to his wrist with a leather strap.

"Well, that didn't work out quite the way I expected," said Melvin, "but never mind. I'll do my best. Lexie, there's some tape on the table. Will you bring it please, if your strength has returned for good?"

Lexie smiled and brought the tape. She watched as Melvin taped his baton together. "Let's try again," he said.

He waved the baton over his tall silk hat and pulled out a blue handkerchief, well almost. It was only half a handkerchief. He tried again and again. Out came half a pink handkerchief tied to half a red handkerchief. Then came a string of half handkerchiefs of varied colors.

"It's no use," said Melvin. "This baton is sick." He examined it. "You children can fix it! Just say the magic word,

Abracadabra, as loudly as you can after I put the broken pieces in my hat. Ready? One, two, three. Go!"

"*Abracadabra*!" resounded through the room.

Melvin put his hand into his hat and withdrew a whole baton. "Thank you! Thank you!" he said. "You are such a good audience I will perform some magic especially for you—if Lexie doesn't take anything."

He guessed cards selected by Lexie from a complete deck, removed more ping pong balls from Lexie's nose, and brought a rabbit from his hat and gave it to Lexie to hold. Then he pulled one dove after another from his hat and then let them fly around the room. He picked up his hat, looked inside it then said, "It's empty folks. That's all."

Loud clapping broke out. Melvin thanked Lexie. She started to return to her seat. "Just a minute, Lexie," said Melvin, "you're taking my props again." Deftly he removed six more ping-pong balls from Lexie's nose and two gold rings from her ears.

This was too much for Lexie. She collapsed into the chair laughing. Bill, Glen, and Debby walked up to meet her and Melvin.

Bill said, "I enjoyed the show. I'll have to try some of those tricks when we get settled in our new home. Now how are you going to get all the birds back?"

"I'll let you into a secret," answered Melvin. "The birds are hungry. Their food is in a hamper at the back of the room. Lexie, do you want to go and open it?"

She did. All the birds flew into it immediately.

"Just close the lid gently," said Melvin. "That's right. Now I can say goodbye and thanks to my assistant. Is there anything else you want to know?"

"Oh, yes!" said Lexie. "Everything!"

"A magician shouldn't give away his secrets. Even if you know how to do a trick it takes a lot of practice to be able to do it yourself." As he talked Melvin packed his props. "Some of my tricks are very old ones. Do you know how Houdini's mother discovered she had a magician in her family?"

The children shook their heads from side to side as they chorused, "No!"

"Pieces of freshly baked cake disappeared even from a locked cupboard."

Lexie asked," How did you take away my strength?"

"I won't tell you. But that magic helped the French government many years ago. One magician was better than an entire army. If you want to know more try looking up magic in an encyclopedia in the ship's library. I've given away too much tonight."

As they returned to their cabin Lexie said to Bill "I wish I knew how he did those tricks."

"Did you see anything hidden under his table?" Bill said. "You probably didn't tie the ropes very tight and he was able to slip out of them."

"I'd like to see you tied up and see how you escape. Oops!" She held on to the cabin door handle as a sudden large swell rocked the great ship. "I'd forgotten we're on the ocean. Anyway, did you notice move one in the Old Grouch game?"

"How'd you figure that?" asked Bill.

"I got Old Grouch to move didn't I? The kids booed him too. Right out of the lounge. He's such a meanie. I'm glad Melvin gave me back my strength. I think I'm going to need it before this journey's over." The great ship creaked a little but settled enough for Lexie to let go of the door-knob and knock firmly.

Bill let go of the handhold.

Their father opened the door. "Both of you look happy," he said. "What happened?"

"The magic show was fun and I was the magician's assistant," said Lexie.

I'm glad you enjoyed it," said Mother. "Now I hope you can settle down and sleep. This will be our first night to sleep on the ocean. We have a waterbed. We'll probably be rocked to sleep like babies."

"You'd better not get to sleep too quickly," said Bill in a whisper to Lexie. "You'd better figure out your next move. You've only got four more in the Old Grouch game."

~5~

Old Grouch
Makes Enemies

"**W**HERE DO YOU THINK Debby and Glen are?" asked Lexie as she left the restaurant.

"Probably sleeping in," answered Bill. "I expect we'll meet them on the Sports Deck. Let's take our photo to the jeweler's first so I can buy my watch. I forgot it yesterday."

The jeweler's shop near the restaurant had one small display window. In it were souvenir type objects: k e y chains, charms, spoons, rings, watches, cufflinks, and tiepins. Lexie noticed that inside, a great variety of clocks could be seen. In response to the bell which tinkled as Lexie and Bill entered, an elderly gentleman with white eyebrows and white hair came through the curtain from an inner room at the other end of the counter.

"Good morning! May I help you?"

"Hello. I want a watch with a sweep second hand, the day, and the date." While Bill selected his watch, Lexie looked at the cuckoo clocks on the wall behind the jeweler.

Just as Bill started to count out his money for his purchase a cuckoo clock started to whirr. Then out popped a cuckoo. Before that cuckoo stopped another started, then another, and another, and another. Lexie watched fascinated as birds of different colors and sizes came out to mark the hour. The clock she liked best had a cuckoo and also dancers who twirled around in time with music.

Mr. McDermitt, the jeweler/photographer, told her, "I sell a lot of cuckoo clocks but you know what? Some people bring them back after a few days and complain. If we are traveling to England they say that the clocks lose an hour a day. If we are on our way to America, they complain the clocks gain an hour a day."

Lexie's forehead creased with a frown. "That's odd! Why would they all lose or gain an hour?" she asked.

Bill butted in, "Don't you remember when we went to Greenwich and straddled the Prime Meridian? Clocks have to be changed an hour after crossing every line of longitude and we go that distance each day. I saw the note about this at the bottom of our daily bulletin."

"Right you are my boy. Just don't come back here complaining if it's your memory that's not working and you didn't turn your watch back one hour."

A late cuckoo sounded.

"Hmm," said Mr. McDermitt. "Now there's a clock that does need fixing or that bird will miss all the worms." He allowed Lexie to watch the cuckoo complete its late calls before removing it from the wall for adjustment. He added, "I have to change each of these cuckoo clocks one hour every day. We are going west now so our time goes backwards."

"I hope you don't get confused. We'll see you at one by my watch to select some prints from our cameras," said Bill.

"If my brother doesn't eat too much for lunch," added Lexie. "Bye for now." The bell on the door tinkled as they left.

"Oops!" said Lexie. "I suddenly felt dizzy. Oh! It happened again. Bill, I think I'm going to faint. I have to hold on to something"

"You're not dizzy, just stupid. The ship just rode some extra large swells."

"What a relief," said Lexie. "There's an awful lot of water out there," she added as she watched the large wake spreading out behind the giant ship. "We have to get a move on. We need to give Buddy some exercise before lunch. Also we won't be able to go swimming this afternoon with Debby and Glen. I'm sure they won't mind, but we'd better find them and let them know. I'll race you to the Sports Deck. Debby and Glen may be there." She now felt quite confident about finding her way around the ship.

Bill soon overtook Lexie. She stuck her tongue out at him as he passed her, and she arrived on the Sports Deck some moments after Bill. He was already talking with Debby and Glen and a group of other children who'd been in the middle of a game.

"Hello," panted Lexie, as she acknowledged the new faces.

Debby introduced the other children.

"Do you want to meet Buddy? We are on our way to feed him and give him exercise," said Lexie.

"Sure," answered Debby. "Are there any other dogs in the kennels?"

"Just six of the cutest poodles you've ever seen, a great, big, enormous Dane, a dark German Shepherd and a St. Bernard," answered Lexie.

"What are we waiting for? Let's go," said Glen.

"We like animals. Can we come too?" asked Norma, one of the new children.

"Of course," said Lexie. "Buddy loves everyone, well almost everyone."

Fortunately few people went to the Upper Deck reserved for animals so the children didn't harm anyone in their rush to see the dogs. When they arrived they all talked at once.

"She's the sweetest?"

"What a darling."

"Sure would scare me if I met that on a street one night."

Bill opened Buddy's kennel. Buddy never could quite wait to get out.

"Buddy, come!" yelled Lexie. "You've got a lot of admirers to see you today." She knelt on the deck to pet Buddy.

Soon many hands wanted a turn to stroke Buddy. He licked a face or hand whenever he got a chance. He also held up his paw to shake hands.

"He is handsome," said Debby as she shook hands with Buddy.

Lexie said, "He is cooped up so much we must give him some exercise. Let's sit around the deck and take turns to call him. We'll see who he'll go to."

The children spread out around the deck and squatted

or sat cross-legged. "Here Buddy! Here Buddy!" yelled the children. Each one trying to yell louder than the others.

Buddy barked, wagged his tail and then ran excitedly to Lexie. "Sit," commanded Lexie. Buddy obeyed immediately.

"Here, Buddy! Here, Buddy!" rang out again

Suddenly a voice thundered across the deck. "What's going on here?"

Buddy was on his way to Bill but froze to the deck at the sound of that voice. Lexie's heart beat faster when she saw it was Old Grouch.

"You kids stay away from my dog," he continued angrily. He strode across the deck toward the St. Bernard. Buddy lay right in his path. Old Grouch made no attempt to go around or over Buddy. He kicked Buddy out of the way.

A gasp escaped the lips of the children.

Buddy whimpered. He'd never been treated like this before. At first Lexie was so shocked she couldn't move. Then she jumped up and rushed to Buddy and rubbed his side in the place where he'd received the blow.

"Come on, Buddy. Let's shake hands. You didn't do anything wrong."

But Buddy, although he'd stopped whimpering, had hurt feelings as well as a hurt body, and wouldn't shake hands.

Meanwhile Old Grouch had inspected the St. Bernard. Again the dog gave no sign of welcome or recognition of Old Grouch.

Old Grouch snarled, " I'm going to get the Kennel Steward. There'll be no more of this. My dog will be a nervous wreck before we get to the dog show in New York." He shook his stick at the unusually quiet children, then stormed off.

Lexie continued to coax Buddy to shake hands. Eventually the Boxer responded.

Lexie said, "Old Grouch is going to be sorry for what he did to Buddy. Now do you believe me, Bill? Old Grouch is a very unpleasant example of a human and he's involved in something bad."

"Well I know what I saw with my own two eyes. He's not going to get away with that. All in favor of teaching Old Grouch to respect animals say 'Aye.'"

"Aye!" came a hearty response.

Bill led Buddy back to his kennel. Then the children stood in a group by the ship's bright yellow funnel with black lines dividing its height in thirds. Bill pointed at the funnel and said, "This funnel makes the *Ocean Queen* recognizable as belonging to the same company as sister ships with those markings. I'll show you my collection of ship photos and flags later but right now I have to eat. I can't be expected to think on an empty stomach. Lexie and I have to get a quick lunch. We won't be able to swim until about three this afternoon. We'll keep thinking about what we'll do about Old Grouch. See you at the pool."

"You can count on me," added Lexie as she patted Buddy in his kennel.

~6~

New Developments

"WHAT TIME IS IT?" Lexie asked Bill.

"One," he answered, "and here comes Mr. McDermitt. At least he keeps time with the watches he sells."

"Hello! Hello! Not getting impatient are you?" Mr. Mc-Dermitt inquired as he unlocked his door.

"I'm always impatient when I'm excited," replied Lexie, but I think I can wait for five more minutes.

Having opened the door to his shop Mr. McDermitt signaled them ahead. Then he re-locked the door. "I've no time for customers in the afternoons. One thing you can't have is interruptions in the darkroom," he said.

"We've just missed the cuckoo clocks," Lexie said.

"Well, here's a timer. Set it for fifty minutes and bring it into the darkroom. We should be finished with your photos by that time if I'm to get prints done for my other customers."

Lexie touched the right number of minutes and spent a few moments trying to find a spot where she could set the timer down on the cluttered workbench.

"Go through that curtain," said Mr. McDermitt. "Okay. Now we get to work. I'll turn on the screen and display all your pictures and you can chose if you want wallet, postcard, or larger size."

My picture of the pilot is good," said Bill, "and I caught him right above his boat."

"So did I," said Lexie but I like the sea gulls best."

Lexie looked then clapped her hand over her mouth to suppress a squeal. "Oh! Bill look. It's Old Grouch." She'd forgotten she'd taken his photo.

Bill glanced over and said, "He really is smiling. Amazing! Maybe you should make a print for him."

"Is he a friend of yours?" Mr. McDermitt asked.

"Oh! No!" answered Lexie with a slight shudder. "Don't make him any bigger. I think he's too big already. There! That's fine," she indicated when the image got down to postcard size as Mr. McDermitt changed it.

A loud ringing interrupted them.

Lexie jumped. "What's that?" she asked.

"Golly! You set the alarm," said Bill.

"Oh! I've been so interested I forgot all about the cuckoo clocks. I'll go out now." Lexie left quickly, all excited.

Some five minutes later Bill and Mr. McDermitt came out of the print room and found Lexie still in the workroom. She stood by the curtained doorway that led into the actual shop. The cuckoos began to call. Lexie changed her weight from one foot to the other and clenched and unclenched her fists, an agonized expression on her face.

"What's the matter?" asked Mr. McDermitt as he plugged in an electric kettle.

"Nothing!" she answered without convincing anyone.

"You were in such a hurry to watch the cuckoos just now," said Bill.

Lexie blurted out, "Old Grouch is looking in through the window."

Mr. McDermitt went into his shop followed by Bill, but Lexie would only look out from the curtain. Standing outside the window was Old Grouch. They looked at him. He returned their gaze for an instant then moved off.

The electric kettle started to whistle. "Come on," said Mr. McDermitt. "Let's have a cuppa while the prints dry." He turned to the table in his workroom and set up two more folding chairs. As they drank tea Mr. McDermitt said, "You've both made a good beginning in the darkroom. Lexie, that man you called Old Grouch was in the first picture you printed, right? "

She nodded yes.

"Is he a friend or has he been bothering you? We can go to the Purser if you like and he will take care of the problem," said Mr. McDermitt.

"Oh! No! He's grumbled at me but I did drop my suitcase on his foot. He kicked my dog on purpose and I'm angry about that. He always seems to be snarling."

"So that's why you call him Old Grouch. He's been in my shop once. I'm trying to remember his name;   i   t definitely wasn't Old Grouch," Mr. McDermitt added with a laugh. "But Old Grouch is easier to remember."

"Did he buy anything?" asked Lexie.

"No. In fact...this is just a secret between ourselves...I

didn't care much for him myself. He acted kind of, well, you know..."Uppity," and definitely with a capital U. There was something odd too. Most people are interested in something made using gems but he only seemed interested in the gems themselves, and far better ones than I have. I told him to shop in New York. My stock seemed far too ordinary for his taste. He did know what he was talking about. "

Lexie looked at Bill and raised her eyebrows.

"Well," said Mr. McDermitt, "I have some other customers who want prints ready by morning. You can carry your pictures in that envelope. If I get rushed I know where to get two good assistants."

"It's been fun," said Lexie. "Thank you and goodbye."

"Thanks a lot," said Bill. "Goodbye."

They lingered on the Promenade Deck a while. "The wind is stronger today," said Lexie as she faced it and her hair blew behind her. "Hold tight to that envelope or our photos will be blown overboard."

As they made their way back to their cabin to leave their photos in a safe place before going swimming with the other children, Lexie said, "I'm even more curious now about Old Grouch. He looks ordinary. He wouldn't stand out in a crowd. His clothes are drab and not particularly classy. His speech definitely doesn't appear to be high class. His cabin is not in the luxury suites. Yet he is interested in very expensive gems. He doesn't look as if he could afford high-priced jewelry in New York. The dog he claims as his own is purebred and a very fine animal. Something in this picture is odd. Just like the man. There's the dog show tonight so I haven't got much time for plans. I haven't made another move yet but I will be-fore this day is over! Trust me."

~7~

Teaching Old Grouch
New Tricks

LEXIE AND BILL RETURNED to the Upper Deck after dinner to feed Buddy and of course give him a few scraps. George the dog trainer and Ben the Kennel Steward were already there.

George said to them, "Are you ready for my show? It will be a great help if you and Ben take charge of the dogs before and after they do their acts and help get them to and from the lounge. You've never been introduced. This is Duke," he said, indicating the Great Dane. "The German Shepherd is Hans. Right here are the poodles: Fifi, Gigi, Migi, Patti, Matti, and Hatti. I wish I could say that St. Bernard is mine. Isn't he a beaut?" He walked towards the dog.

"You'd better stay away from him," cautioned Ben. "He's a fine dog but his owner is rather touchy and gets upset if anyone goes near that St. Bernard. Which reminds me, Lexie and Bill, I received a complaint today about a lot of children causing a disturbance up here and making this St. Bernard nervous."

Lexie spoke indignantly, "Well, what a nerve he's got. We were playing with Buddy but no dogs were upset until that man arrived."

"I bet he didn't tell you what he did to Buddy," added Bill, his voice rising in anger.

"Now take it easy," answered Ben. "I know you're a couple of nice kids and I can't imagine you hurting any animal. Just don't bring other children up here. This deck is strictly for animals and their owners. I'll do my best to keep the peace."

George said, "It's time to get ready for the show. With the money we earn in New York I'll be able to buy my own St. Bernard. Let's go. Who'll take Duke?"

"I will. I will," said Lexie jumping up as she spoke.

George slipped a leash on the Great Dane and passed him over to Lexie. "Hold on now," he advised her.

Duke proceeded to give Lexie's face long, slow licks while he had one paw on each of her shoulders.

Lexie collapsed in giggles and rolled on the deck. Duke thought this some new kind of game. He straddled her and with his long tongue hanging out licked her more and more.

"Crummy! You're scaring me you great, big, enormous brute." Lexie laughed. "Watch out or I may lick you back."

George had finished attaching leashes to all the dogs. He and Ben held the poodles. Bill took the German Shepherd.

"Now, Lexie! Now, Duke! Don't make your own show.

Come on," called Bill as George and Ben walked toward the stairs they needed to take to get to the lounge. Their attention was caught by a sudden, loud bark.

"Oh dear," said Lexie. "Buddy wants to come too. He knows some tricks we taught him at home George. Can he be in your show?"

"It's O.K. with me if you put him through his paces," answered George.

Lexie excitedly got Buddy on a leash. "Come on boy. We'll show 'em."

Duke and Buddy sniffed each other. Then Lexie pulled on their leashes and she, Buddy, and Duke followed George, Ben, and Bill.

A crowd had already gathered in the lounge. Everyone had seen the show announced in the daily bulletin. The chattering stopped and exclamations of admiration were heard as the perfectly white, well-groomed poodles entered. As Lexie came in with the Great Dane, people on the aisle seats drew back involuntarily, amazed at his size.

George whispered to Lexie and Bill, "Do you want to start with Buddy?"

"Sure," answered Bill. "Buddy knows the routine. I'll take him outside while Lexie explains it to the audience." He handed Hans over to George, then took Buddy from Lexie.

After Bill and Buddy left, Lexie turned to the audience and said, "If you choose a place for me to hide, you can call Bill to return and our Boxer will find me at once. Where shall I hide?"

"Behind the couch," called out a voice.

"Okay." Lexie hid behind it making sure no part of her body extended beyond the couch.

Ben recalled Bill and Buddy. Once inside the door Bill removed Buddy's leash.

Immediately Buddy ran to the couch, barked, and went behind it. Lexie came out smiling, patting Buddy's head. "Good dog. Good dog," she said, and handed Buddy a dog biscuit as the audience applauded.

"Here Buddy," called Bill. He put him back on the leash and said, "We'd better do it again so that you know he can ALWAYS find Lexie and that it wasn't an accident." He left the lounge with Buddy at his heels. As soon as the door closed a voice yelled, "Hide in the closet!"

"Okay," said Lexie. She hid behind the coats hanging there and pulled the door almost closed, but again taking care that no part of her could be seen outside the closet.

Ben called Bill to come and find Lexie.

As soon as Buddy was released he ran unerringly to the closet and barked. Lexie came out and gave Buddy another treat amid more applause.

"There's no place I could hide that Buddy couldn't find me," boasted Lexie. Then she added with a smile, "As long as I have my ultrasonic whistle." She withdrew the whistle on a chain around her neck. Lexie and Bill gave a short bow and stepped aside for George to introduce himself and his dogs.

First George introduced the poodles. "They may be small," he said "but when they operate together they make quite a team of strength." He'd kept them on their leashes. "One. Two. Three. Go!" They ran around him until his legs were firmly tied together. Then they pulled and George fell backwards on the floor.

"Gosh!" said Lexie. "That was no accident when Mrs.

Bryant hit the deck. They've been trained to do that. I wonder if she knows?"

"She'd be furious with George if she did," answered Bill. "But what made them do it to her. Nobody had said, "One, two, three. Go!"

"Animals are sensitive to tones of voice. Maybe they didn't like being called awful creatures," said Lexie.

George called Bill to help remove and untangle the leashes. Then he picked up the Toy, signaled with his hand, and the other five poodles began to run clockwise in a circle. "Do your stuff, Migi," commanded George as he placed her facing counterclockwise on the back of one of the other running poodles. She ran over the backs and heads of all the other poodles until George ordered, "Stop!" Migi jumped down and stood still by him.

"Jump!" was the next command George gave. Five poodles played leapfrog over Migi. When George stopped that game the poodles lined up in front of him with Migi at the end of the line. George tossed a dog biscuit to each of the five larger poodles. Then he placed one on the floor in front of the leader. Migi ran under all the poodles and slid under the chin of the first poodle just in time to make off with the treat.

During the laughing and clapping Lexie came forward to help replace the leashes. George took Hans from Bill and led the German Shepherd to one side of the lounge. "Sit," George ordered. The dog obeyed. George added, "Stay!" Then he walked to the back of the room.

Ben came over to the dog holding a juicy piece of meat. "Here boy! Here boy! This treat is for you." Ben spoke in a very friendly, coaxing voice.

Hans looked at the tempting piece of meat. His nose twitched a little. However he stayed completely still no matter how many times Ben repeated, "Here boy! Here boy! This treat is for you."

George called from the back of the room, "Good dog! Good dog! Come." Hans ran to him instantly to be rewarded with a tasty treat and affectionate pats. As George and Hans walked to the front of the room he said, "I'd like a lady to volunteer to walk across the room holding her purse. I promise she won't get hurt."

Someone stepped forward. Ben now took on the role of a thief. He walked toward the woman and as he passed her grabbed her purse and ran.

"Hans get that man," ordered George.

The German Shepherd moved so fast that even though Ben had been warned beforehand, his face showed surprise. "Help!" Ben yelled as the dog grabbed the sleeve of his coat and pulled him to the floor.

George told the crowd, "Hans will hold on until I give him different instructions. If anyone is holding a gun, Hans is trained to go for the gun hand. As long as the person believes he is caught Hans won't harm him. I wouldn't advise anyone to think he can get away."

George then said, "Okay, Hans. Release," to the obvious relief of Ben who now felt able to stand up again. He was perspiring slightly, and mopped his brow with a handkerchief as the audience applauded. George returned the purse to the rightful owner.

Lexie whispered to Bill, "How about asking George to let us borrow Hans to make Old Grouch hit the deck? Also I would be helped to stay upright when we hit another swell like this one if I had Hans to hold on to. Wowy! Zowy!"

"Is this ship creaking or are your bones making that noise?" joked Bill. "This is fun but I could use a seat belt. Look at the ocean through the porthole. Perhaps you'd better not. Now what were you asking before King Neptune startled us? Oh! About Hans. George would get into trouble if he loaned us a dog. We have to take action ourselves."

Now the show involved the Great Dane. He'd been trained to obey visual signals. George removed something from his pocket. It turned out to be an expanding walking stick. He looked at Duke then pointed the stick at Lexie and Bill. Duke walked over to them. Then George moved the stick in a circular motion. Duke rolled over on the floor like a puppy. Then George touched his right shoulder. Duke placed his paws on the spot. Next George raised the stick in a threatening manner.

The Great Dane leaped toward George.

The crowd gasped in horror to see so huge an animal attack a person. The gasp changed to laughter as Duke completed his leap with a loving lick.

As far as George was concerned the dogs had done enough but the audience was not willing that the show should end yet. George took a firm stand. "That's enough for them. It is important not to overwork animals."

But George didn't have the last word.

Lexie led the procession of dogs from the lounge. George waved goodbye to the audience. The people rose and followed. They chanted, "More! More! More!"

Suddenly Lexie stopped. There, right ahead, sat Old Grouch in a deck chair. A blanket covered him due to the breeze coming off the Atlantic Ocean. Lexie looked over her shoulder. She couldn't go back because there were too many adults and children that way. No alternative being possible she had to pass Old Grouch. Then she had an idea for her next move in the Old Grouch game. "If only I can get his attention," she muttered.

She started to whistle. She slowed down. With her head held high and a cocky upward tilt of her nose, she stopped her tune, wrinkled her nose, and called in a louder than normal voice, "Duke! Whew! Something around here stinks! It's terrible! What is it?" She'd shouted loud enough to disturb Old Grouch. She hoped he would give his usual reaction. Nothing happened. Didn't he hear anything when he sat reading? she thought to herself. She'd have to do something else.

She bumped his deck chair, and just as she'd hoped, it caused his usual reaction.

Old Grouch looked up and yelled, "It's YOU again! A ship is a very small place when there's a nuisance like you on board." He raised his walking stick and shook it at her in a threatening manner.

Duke saw the signal. To him it meant only one thing. He went for Old Grouch the way he had been trained to do on seeing the raised arm holding a stick. His lunge forward jerked the leash from Lexie's hand. She let go of her Boxer's leash and Buddy followed Duke.

The German Shepherd, Hans, sensed excitement and escaped from Bill to follow Buddy and Duke. The poodles didn't want to be left out of any fun and so they surprised George with one big pull together and took off after Duke, Buddy, and Hans, leaving George speechless!

Old Grouch leapt from the deck chair as the Great Dane landed on it. He dashed through a door a short way along the deck. The dogs gave chase followed by Lexie, Bill, George, and Ben. George recovered his voice enough to shout the names of his usually well-behaved dogs. Apparently they couldn't hear him above the noise of the clanking metal leashes, Old Grouch's screams, the wind, and the clamoring of the people crowding in behind him to see this unforeseen part of the show and still chanting, "More! More! More!"

The door led into the galley. Just as a pastry cook concentrated on the finishing touches to a beautiful eleven-tier angel cake with lemon frosting, he was swept off his feet by the sudden onslaught of Old Grouch and the dogs. The cake wobbled for a moment and then toppled over.

"*Mon Dieu*! (My God)" gasped the French cook.

"Get me out of here," screamed Old Grouch, trying to keep the dogs at bay with a cupboard door.

"Willingly!" screamed the furious cook as he began throwing eggs at him and yelling, "*Maudit soit tu!* (Curses on you)" Several eggs smashed on the shiny, copper-bottomed pots and pans on the wall, but most of them hit Old Grouch. He took off for another door at the end of the galley. The dogs, distracted for a while to taste the broken eggs and angel cake, followed. So did more eggs.

The cook began to cry as he looked at the broken remains of his masterpiece scattered all over the floor.

Lexie, Bill, George, and Ben followed in hot pursuit calling all the dogs by name. They were just in time to see Old Grouch going out the far door with the Great Dane almost close enough to give the big lick that would be the end of his trick.

The cook rushed to lock the galley door to prevent further intrusions just in time to keep out the crowd clamoring, "More! More! More!"

The kitchen floor had now become hazardous. Lexie stepped into some cake, frosting, and broken eggs, and skidded across the floor, followed by Bill, Ben, and George hydroplaning in her tracks. They all ended up in a heap at the far door.

The maddened cook seeing his smashed cake and the frosted floor in his once immaculate kitchen, yelled, "Out! Out! Out!" He grabbed more eggs and threw them with accuracy.

"Yuck!" said Bill, as egg dripped down his face. "Let's get out of here."

They all got on the other side of the door as fast as they could just as the cook collapsed in a faint behind his worktable.

Ben spoke up. "We can catch them now. There's no other way out. This leads to a small deck where cooks and other kitchen workers take their coffee and tea breaks."

When they came out on the deck they saw the frightened Old Grouch had somehow hoisted himself up and sat on the railing. The Great Dane couldn't quite reach to give that lick but he had his paws up on Old Grouch. All the other dogs yapped and barked at his feet.

Then terrified Old Grouch swung his feet over the railing and held on by only his hands. Lexie, Bill, Ben, and George rushed to the railing to help him but arrived too late. They heard a very loud scream, a very long scream, but it sounded further and further away. A splash brought people to all the decks on that side of the ship. They all watched horrified for a moment.

Ben immediately threw a life belt to Old Grouch and called, "Man overboard." He broke the glass on the emergency call button for instant contact with the Captain. Then he ran for help.

Lexie felt worried. She had only meant to scare Old Grouch. This had gone further than she expected. The vacation atmosphere had changed to tension. She couldn't see if Old Grouch had grabbed on to the life belt. Emergency procedures had already started. The great ship reduced speed. At the same time the stern was swung away from the man in the water so that he would not be caught in the propellers. Lexie wondered how long a person could survive in such cold water without a wet suit.

The lifeboat drill had not seemed very real to Lexie. Now she watched as a lifeboat was slowly lowered to the ocean. She saw a few sailors on board, then she heard the motor start, and watched as the very small looking lifeboat, now that it was no longer over the deck but on the vast ocean, set off to find Old Grouch.

"I'm glad some people know exactly what to do," she said. "But we've gone so far past him. Oh! We're turning in a circle."

"A ship this big can't turn very fast," explained George. "It must be slowed down gradually and takes about a mile to come to a stop. You might as well help me get these sticky leashes sorted out for the right animal while we backtrack to...what did you call him?"

"Oh! We don't know his name," volunteered Lexie. As they regained control of the animals, Lexie thought it better not to mention the nickname, Old Grouch.

Some cheering broke out from the passengers crowding

the railings on every deck. Lexie, Bill, and George looked out over the sea to where they saw sailors hauling the wet and frightened Old Grouch into the lifeboat. He appeared to be shaken, very shaken, but not visibly hurt. Lexie gave a sigh of relief.

The lifeboat and its passengers were hauled back up on deck with winches. Lexie saw Old Grouch's walking stick was still attached to his wrist! "He doesn't want to be parted from that cane," commented Lexie quietly to Bill. "I wonder why?"

Two sailors appeared with a stretcher and despite his protestations Old Grouch was taken to the ship's hospital to be checked by the ship's doctor. The great ship returned to its normal course.

"Oh dear!" said George. "Maybe my wife is right. Perhaps I should give up my dogs and do something more relaxing."

"Well don't relax yet," advised Bill. "There's only one way off this deck and that is through the galley. Who's going first? I bet that cook is still angry about his spoiled cake."

Lexie said, "Let's crawl through. The cupboards will hide us most of the time. Follow me very, very, very quietly. Bill, you'd better stay way behind me because if I see your egg soaked hair and face I just might not be able to keep from laughing. Let's go." She walked as far as the door that had protected them from the cook then got down on her hands and knees. She opened the door a little and looked in. "It's okay! He's on the phone. Now follow me. Shhh."

Lexie with the Boxer and the Great Dane, Bill with the German Shepherd, George and the six once-white poodles, crawled across the floor through the cake, eggs, eggshells, and frosting. The dogs ate as much as they could while having to keep up with the others.

As they got closer to the phone they heard the cook saying, "No. Tell the doctor I want to see him today. I can't do anymore cooking. I'm having hallucinations. I thought I saw dogs and people running around in here. And my beautiful cake, she is ruined! And my kitchen floor is a mess!"

Lexie had come to a halt. There were no more cupboards between them and the door. The dogs continued to eat. The Great Dane was surprised when on lowering his head to get a tasty morsel of cake the Toy poodle slid under his chin and swallowed the delicious portion.

Lexie crept across the open space. She couldn't open the door. The cook had locked it. She would have to stand up to slide the bolt. She signaled to the others to come quickly as she stood up and opened the door.

A wail came from the cook. "Oh! No-o-o! I'm seeing them again. Tell the doctor to come and get me! *Vite! Vite!* (Quick! Quick!)" Once more he fainted. The phone swung over the cook's head as three people and nine dogs hurriedly left the galley and returned to the Upper Deck. Fortunately most of the passengers, drawn to the railings by the dramatic scene of rescuing the man overboard, had stayed to visit and discuss the event. They didn't notice six egg spattered and frosted poodles, a German Shepherd, a Great Dane, and three people slinking by unobtrusively.

Ben had already arrived on the Upper Deck. He had just put a bowl of food in with the St. Bernard. He turned as he heard footsteps approaching. "Oh boy!" exclaimed Ben when he saw the messy group. "All of you need to be hosed down. We'll have to watch out for the rest of this trip. That man is furious. He has no broken bones or anything other than a few bruises visible but the doctor gave him a tranquilizer and insists that he stays under observation for twenty four hours to be sure no damage has been done to his soft internal organs."

Lexie said, "I wouldn't want to be around when that tranquilizer wears off. I hope he isn't hurt badly because I want to have a jolly good laugh. I do hope he hurts as much as Buddy did."

Buddy gave Duke a big lick. Then another and another.

"Isn't he being nice to Duke," asked Lexie? "Buddy has good manners. Do you think that's his way of thanking Duke?"

"Don't be nutty, little sister," answered Bill. "He just likes the taste of the frosting on Duke's coat."

"Anyway, Bill," she whispered "that was my second move. Three to go for checkmate."

A sudden deep pitch of the ship surprised them.

"Whoa there!" shrieked Lexie. "Gosh! I'd forgotten about the ocean after getting past that cook."

"The ocean won't let you do that for long," said Ben. "Hmm! I don't like the look of the sky or the size of the swells. We'd better get these dogs cleaned up and back in the kennels. It looks to me like trouble's brewing and we're heading right into it."

George nodded his head in agreement. "You've spoken the truth. I have to go face my wife. I'll never live this down. I've always told her I have those dogs under control at all times." As he cleaned up the dogs, assisted by Lexie,

Bill, and Ben, George continued to shake his head in disbelief.

Lexie said, "We'd better go to the showers and go swimming before going back to our cabin and get cleaned up before our parents see us looking like this."

As they left the deck, George repeated mournfully, "Yes. Trouble's brewing and I'm heading right into it."

~ 8 ~

Lexie Finds a Clue

L EXIE WOKE UP AND felt confused. What's happening? she thought. Am I dreaming? As she became
more alert she realized this was no dream. The whole ship
shook and shuddered. It tipped from side to side and up
and down.

"Is anyone awake?" she called anxiously.

"Yes," answered Bill, Mother, and Father in unison.

Father switched on a light. As he did so he said, "We're
not likely to get any more sleep in this storm. We may as
well get up. It's a little after six."

Getting dressed was difficult since one hand had to be
used to hold on to something firm. A sudden lurch of the
ship threw them all in a heap in one corner.

"Crummy!" screamed Lexie. "I'm getting back into bed
to finish dressing."

Mother, holding carefully to her bed, passed a bag of

gingersnaps and said, "Eat these for breakfast today. You may want to skip eggs and bacon and milk until this storm is over. Drink plenty of water though."

"I'd like a cup of water," said Lexie.

"Here you are dear," said Mother.

Lexie took a sip but an upward movement of the ship sloshed the water all over her. She joined in Bill's laughter as she mopped up her face, her T-shirt and jeans, and the floor. The rest of the family, being warned, managed their drinks on a downward motion of the ship.

Someone will have to give Buddy gingersnaps," Father said. "We may as well put on our coats and all go to see him. He may be upset by this storm."

"I bet he's scared," said Lexie.

"Well, hop to it and let's go," said Mother. "You children are not to go up on deck alone in this kind of weather. It isn't safe."

They went out of the cabin one at a time and grabbed for the closest handhold on the wall. "I wondered what all these bars on the walls were for," said Lexie. "Whee! This is all the fun of the fair rolled into one ride."

"Rolled is the word," added Bill. He held tight as the wall where he was holding seemed to be coming on top of him.

Lexie was pushed into the wall on the opposite side of the corridor. She screamed, "Wow! Is this ship ever going to be upright again! It would be difficult to have a dog show or magic show in this weather."

Normal walking was completely out of the question. Lexie and Bill made more of a game out of it by going from side to side as they progressed slowly down the corridor. They didn't have time for bickering. They almost bumped into a very pale steward hurrying on his way with medicine to help those already struck with seasickness from the violent movements of the ship.

When they got to the stairs it became even more fun for them. "Eee-e-e-h! This is like going up a flight of stairs with unexpected steps missing," said Lexie.

"Yes," said Bill. "Then just as I get used to stepping farther than usual, the floor comes up and hits me with a jolt. This must be like riding a bucking bronco. Somebody should tell King Neptune we have no plans to become cowboys in America."

"Walking on the pavement will suit me," said Lexie.

Clinging to the banister Bill said, "Don't forget, Glen said the pavement is for cars in America. We have to stay on the sidewalk."

"Ugh!" groaned Lexie as a downward plunge of the ship left her stomach high above her head. It was also her reply to Bill about her worries of language mix-ups. But nobody can feel low for long during a storm on an ocean.

"Whee!" yelled Lexie with an upward surge of the ship. "Do they charge extra for this fun ride?"

They were all out of breath by the time they got to the top of the stairs. Father called to them, "Wait a minute. It probably won't be possible to talk when we come out on the deck. The wind will carry our voices away. Keep together and hold tight to something or somebody all the time."

When they came out on deck Lexie couldn't believe this was where they'd played games or sat sunning themselves in deck chairs. The ocean now gave a display of power. It was exhilarating. Rain slashed across Lexie's face driven by a forceful wind. She saw waves of terrifying height come crashing into the sides of the ship. She felt glad to be on a huge ship. She remembered the words of the Captain that he'd crossed the Atlantic many times without a mishap, so she figured he knew what to do. There didn't seem to be any danger of waves coming over the deck—except in Bill's stories. She thought of the sailors who braved such storms in much smaller ships—the *Kon Tiki* expedition on rafts, the Pilgrims, the Vikings, and Christopher Columbus—all who had crossed oceans so many years ago without modern communications.

Lexie had been so lost in her own thoughts that she didn't realize she'd dropped back until Mother said, "Lexie! Move along and keep up with Dad and Bill." She found it easy to hold onto the railing around the deck. The roll to each side did stop just AFTER the moment she thought the ship couldn't recover and stay afloat any longer. She caught up with Bill at the last flight of stairs. The Upper Deck gave a tremendous view of the ocean.

"It's awesome!" she commented. Buddy whimpered. He looked confused and frightened. Lexie's attention was given to Buddy at once. "Let me give him a gingersnap or two." Nobody challenged her statement. "Here boy!" she said as she gently stroked her pet. "There won't be any more games until this storm is over. You may be able to stand on your four legs but we can't manage very well on two! We can't let you out to play. Here are some ginger-snaps for your treat. We'll come back often today and give you more."

None of the dogs acted at ease. They whimpered and

whined from time to time. Some shivered. Lexie wondered if this was due to fright or cold. Hans's hair stood on end. "I'm glad we gave Buddy gingersnaps every day. Look at the poor St. Bernard, lying in its own vomit. Let's go see if Old Grouch is out of the hospital."

Father took them by their arms and guided them back the way they'd just come.

When they got to the shelter of the main staircase Mother ordered, "Back to our cabin and change out of these soaked clothes."

"We had such trouble getting into them," groaned Lexie. "Couldn't we find the owner of the St. Bernard first? We know his cabin is on B level."

"Okay," said Mother, "but don't be long or you'll catch pneumonia in these cold wet clothes."

Lexie and Bill took off from the staircase at B level and bounced and tumbled their way to cabin B22. Bill went to knock, but held his hand back at the sound of a groan. Another groan followed and yet another. Lexie and Bill exchanged looks.

"Perhaps he got hurt badly from that fall," said Lexie.

"The doctor wouldn't have let him out of the hospital if that were so," replied Bill. "We'd better do something," said Lexie.

Bill knocked. Another groan sounded through the door. Then they heard something that might have been "Come in."

Bill turned the doorknob and they both looked in hesitantly. There lay Old Grouch in his bed. His pale green face matched his pajamas.

"I'm dying," moaned Old Grouch

"You're not dying. You're seasick," said Lexie, hoping he was too sick to remember his last encounter with her. "Do you have any pills or gingersnaps for seasickness?"

"No-o-o-o-o," he groaned.

"I'll ring your bell for a steward." Bill's action matched his words.

"The reason we came," Lexie tried to get in between his groans, "is to tell you your dog is sick."

"You kids...groan...stay away...groan...from that dog."

A knock on the door announced the arrival of the steward. He'd come prepared with medicine. "This is a bad one," he said.

Lexie thought at first he meant Old Grouch, then she realized he meant the storm.

"Here you are, Mr. Sanders. Just take two of these and rest a while. If these don't help the doctor can give you a shot. You'll feel better too if you can get up on deck as soon as possible for some fresh air. It's very hot down here. Many vents have had to be closed due to the waves."

Lexie watched with interest as Old Grouch (Mr. Sanders didn't suit him at all, she thought) sat up, leaning on one elbow, to take the pills. The water splashed over him as it had done to her as the ship gave another huge plunge and shudder. Trying not to giggle, Lexie signaled to Bill that it was time for them to leave. She saw Old Grouch had no thought for the St. Bernard.

As they left Old Grouch in the steward's care, Lexie no longer squealed with the motion of the *Ocean Queen*. She was too concerned about the dog. She said, "We'd better find Ben. He'll know what to do for the animals."

At the Purser's Office a call was placed for them to get

the Kennel Steward. "What can I do for you?" they soon heard Ben say.

"The St. Bernard is very sick and Old...er...Mr. Sanders is sick too and can't get to him. We've just come from his cabin to see if you can help," Lexie hastily explained, hoping to imply that Old Grouch wanted help for the dog he claimed to be his.

"I've been helping other stewards since we struck this storm around five this morning, So many people are sick, including stewards, I haven't had time to get to the dogs. They looked uncomfortable but not ill when I looked in on them earlier. How's Buddy?"

"He's frightened but not sick," said Lexie. "The St. Bernard is awfully sick. Shall we come with you in case you need another pair of hands?"

"Yes, if you're both well enough."

"We're fine," said Bill. "Our mother makes us eat gingersnaps every day."

"Hold tight," were Ben's last words as they came out on the deck and once again battled the wind, the rain, and the convulsions of the ship.

When they reached the dogs they called a greeting to Buddy but went straight to the St. Bernard. "Oh boy! What a mess he's in," said Ben sympathetically. "I did suggest Mr. Sanders give the dog something to prevent this but he didn't think it necessary. Well, let's get on with it. First I'll slip this cloth around his mouth and knot it behind his head... there...just to make sure he doesn't snap at any of us."

All the time he talked he also worked. "Now I'll give him an injection. He'll be quite drowsy and easy to handle in a few minutes. While that takes effect I'll get a hose, bucket, sponge, and some towels and gloves. Bill you can lend a hand. Just hold tight to something as you walk."

While Ben and Bill went to get the equipment, Lexie stroked the sick dog's back. "You'll soon be feeling better," she murmured.

When Ben and Bill returned, Ben said, "Bill, if you'll help me drag him out of here we can soon hose out the mess. Then we can clean him."

"While you do that I'll get his fur cleaned up," said Lexie, as she put on latex gloves.

Ben handed her a bucket of water and a large sponge. Now the dog was sleepy enough for Ben to remove the muzzle. Lexie tenderly cleaned the mussed up fur. Bill and Ben worked together.

Lexie said to the St. Bernard as if he could understand, "I'll have to remove your collar to clean you up properly. Now if I can just raise your head a little...I'll wipe this side of you...there. You look a little better and you smell a whole lot better."

Ben and Bill had almost finished cleaning and drying the kennel. Lexie picked up the dog's collar to replace it. Something caught her attention. She examined the collar carefully. Her heart beat faster. She looked around to see if she'd been observed but nobody was watching. Quickly she replaced the collar.

Ben helped her move and turn the dog to wipe his other side. When the dog was clean and safely back in its kennel, Lexie tugged at Ben's arm. "Ben" she said, "please don't tell Mr. Sanders we helped take care of his dog. O.K?"

"I think he'd be pleased to have such good help while he's too sick to do anything himself," said Ben.

"Just don't mention us to him," said Lexie. When they got to the stairs Lexie whispered to Bill, "I'm so excited. I found something interesting!"

~9~

Bill Is Interested

"**B**ILL, YOU CAN'T SAY I'm imagining anything now," said Lexie. "Listen. When I took that dog's collar off I felt something hard on the underside. I only got a quick look but I saw the collar is made of two strips of leather, hand sewn together, and there's DEFINITELY something in between them. The leather has been hollowed out a bit. It's very thin where the hard lumps are on the underside. The top looks quite normal. There is nothing unusual about the collar."

"Maybe you have stumbled on something after all," Bill said.

Lexie glowed. Had she got Bill's interest at last? Then she wondered about his use of the word "stumbled". Bill could never acknowledge she figured things out. However, she asked, "What should we do about it, Bill?"

"Remember it's your move. You'd better move fast."

"While Old Grouch is sick we'll have a good chance to go back and get the collar for evidence," said Lexie. "Ben will still be busy helping with the sick passengers. But we do have to go back to our cabin and change our wet clothes or Mum, I mean Mom, will have a fit!"

Bill stated, "We could ask Dad if we can borrow a razor blade. Then we could cut a few stitches in the collar and look inside."

"O-o-o-ps!" Lexie cried out as she grabbed for a handrail.

Bill, also holding tight to another handrail, said, " Either we are getting out of the storm or the storm has died down a lot. We're not moving so drastically now."

"We'd better hope it keeps up long enough to keep Old Grouch in his bed, while we investigate," said Lexie.

They started down the stairs with only a little difficulty, unlike their bucking bronco experience this morning. Then they met Father on his way up.

"Hello," said Lexie.

"Where have you two been?" responded Father. "Mum's so worried about you. I've already been up to the animal deck twice and walked along the corridor on B level twice also."

"We had to find the Kennel Steward, Ben, because the St. Bernard's owner is sick too," answered Lexie." We must have just missed you each time because we have only been in the corridor on B level and on Upper Deck."

"We'll hurry back now," added Bill, "so that Mom can stop worrying about us. By the way, I'd like to use one of your razor blades. Some stitches have come undone in the strap of my camera case. If I cut out the old thread I can fix it with a few new stitches."

"Well, that doesn't sound like you, Bill," his surprised Father replied, "however, you may have a blade as soon as this storm is over. You might cut yourself badly right now. I'm going to the Purser's office and make inquiries about the storm. Tell Mum I won't be long."

Lexie looked crestfallen. Once her Father was out of range of hearing her, she said to Bill, "Now what will we do? AFTER the storm is over will be too late to look inside that collar."

Bill clapped his hand on his forehead and said, "What's the matter with me? All we have to do is go to the store and get a pocketknife."

Lexie's worried look vanished. They bounced their way along the passage leading to their cabin with only an occasional need to grab a handrail. They entered quietly so as not to disturb Mother.

Mother sat up a bit and leaning on one elbow said, "I thought you'd gone overboard. I worry about you in this storm. What took so long?"

"We'll tell you later. We have to find the Kennel Steward now, but he's helping with the sick people and the dogs today. I hope you feel better soon," said Bill.

"Hang your wet clothes in the bathroom. There's far less rolling now and the movement side to side is almost pleasant," said Mother.

"You're right," said Lexie. She whispered to Bill, "Hurry!" Turning to Mother, she said, "Goodbye Mum, I mean Mom. We hope you feel better soon."

Lexie and Bill dashed down the corridor barely touching the handrails, not clinging to them as they had to do that morning. On the stairs they encountered their father.

"Hello again," he said. "You do look better. I've got good

news. The Captain said we'd be out of the storm in half an hour."

"Oh!" said Lexie. "We've got to go. Goodbye." She dashed up the stairs. Bill went to overtake her but a sudden lurch of the ship threw him off balance. He stumbled and fell in a heap on the landing.

"Are you all right?" Father called as he hurried up the stairs to where Bill lay still.

"Say something," yelled Lexie."

"Yes. I'll make it," said Bill getting up slowly.

"You'd better come back to the cabin and let me check you," said Father.

"No, Dad! Okay?"

"No, Bill," replied Father firmly. "Back to the cabin."

Lexie and Bill exchanged looks of dismay. *Parents!* thought Lexie. *Of all the luck. Just because Bill has to be first for everything.*

"Ouch," yelled Bill as his father took him by the arm to guide him back to the cabin.

"Sorry, son."

Lexie sighed and followed them.

"In you go, Bill, and take off your shirt," Father ordered. Then he addressed Mother. "The good news is that we'll be out of the storm in a half-hour. The bad news is Bill fell on the stairs. I'm just going to look at the damages."

"Are you hurting much, Bill?" asked Mother.

"No. I've been trying to tell Dad I'm fine! Really."

"Well...no bones are broken. No skin torn. But your back and left arm are quite scraped and red. You'll probably have quite a few bruises. Maybe I'd better take you to the ship's doctor."

"Oh! No!" groaned Bill.

"There's witch hazel in the first aid case on top of the suitcases," said Mother. "That should be enough."

"I'll get it," said Lexie. She tried hard not to let her face show annoyance at yet another delay. She rushed the witch hazel to her father.

As Father carefully applied the cool liquid he said, "I can't understand why you children rush about so. You've got nothing to do all day except eat, play games, swim, or just laze around. Okay. That'll do for now. I'll check it later."

Bill hurriedly put on his shirt as he made his way to the door. Lexie almost stepped on his heels in her haste. As they left, Mother called, "Bill!"

He poked his head back around the door. He tried not to be rude but he almost screamed, "WHAT?"

"Tuck your shirt in BEFORE you leave dear," said Mother. "You're in a public space once you're out of the cabin. There is a difference between casual and sloppy."

Bill resisted the urge to tell his mother that the American boys all wore their shirts outside their trousers. He was in too much of a hurry to discuss different customs. Obediently he rammed his shirt in.

A nod from his mother and a "That's better" indicated he could go. He left with a sigh.

Lexie and Bill tore along the corridor. "We'll never have enough time now," said Lexie.

"Gosh. Dad thinks we've got nothing to do!" Bill said as they entered the shop. He decided a Swiss Army knife would be best for the job. Then they rushed to the Upper Deck to find out the mystery of the dog's collar..

Buddy barked a welcome. He seemed a lot better. Lexie gave him a quick stroke on the head. "We've urgent work to do. We'll play later when the storm is over."

Bill said, "I'll keep watch and warn you if Old Grouch comes this way. Now hurry."

Lexie had already approached the St. Bernard. "He's still sleepy from the medicine." She stroked the beautiful dog's head once. Lexie unbuckled the collar and gently pulled it out of the kennel. Carefully she cut the stitches between the two pieces of leather.

"The coast is still clear but you'd better get a move on," Bill called.

She shook the opened part over her hand. Nothing came out. "I'll have to cut some more." She cut a couple more stitches then she pried the leather apart and out came a... "Crummy!" she yelled to Bill. "Come and look. This must be a diamond. Why would anyone hide a piece of glass in their dog's collar?"

"Just hurry and get that collar back on the dog. We can look and talk later."

Lexie put the Swiss Army knife back in the box and then slipped it and the diamond into her zippered pocket. She then lifted the head of the St. Bernard just enough to slip the collar around his neck. Then she secured it.

"Quick! Someone is coming," whispered Bill. "It's some-one with a stick. I can hear it tapping. We mustn't let Old Grouch see us here."

"I'm done," said Lexie.

The footsteps and tapping stopped.

Bill signaled to Lexie with his finger pressed on his lips. He peeked over the stairs then withdrew immediately. He nodded to the far side of the deck and indicated with his arm for Lexie to follow him.

"We can't go down the steps," whispered Bill. "Old Grouch has sat down in a deckchair just below them."

"What will we do now?" gasped Lexie.

"I'll see if I can climb over the divider going port to starboard. There's an area like a cyclone fence. I think I could lower myself to the bottom. It's only a few feet then to the deck below. I could jump."

Lexie lay on the deck trembling. She hated climbing fences. Then Bill called, "It's fine. You can do it too."

Lexie looked down at him. "It's too far. Your legs are longer than mine."

Bill called, "You'd better hurry up and decide. Come this way or you have to go down the steps and pass Old Grouch."

"Oh dear. I hear him coming up the steps."

"Then act fast. Jump!"

Lexie scrambled over the railing of the fenced area. She looked down. Her eyes opened wider with horror. "It's much too far!"

"Oh! Come on! Don't act like a stupid girl. I'll catch you. Hang from the top and move one hand at a time down the fencing."

Lexie followed Bill's directions as far as hanging by her hands, but that was as far as she'd go. "Crummy! It's too far! I just can't do it," she said, turning her head to look down.

Bill jumped up and grabbed her ankles. She screamed as they hit the deck together.

"You shouldn't have done that," she stormed at Bill.

"Quiet," snapped Bill. "We must walk calmly away from here. Don't draw any more attention to yourself. Now that it's stopped raining many passengers are coming out on the decks for fresh air. We must blend in and do as they do."

They walked to the bow of the ship. Lexie cupped her chin in her hands and leaned on the railing. She watched the churning waves. "The ocean has calmed down a lot compared with this morning," she commented, "but my stomach is doing flip-flops for a different reason now. I'm wondering if we should take the diamond to the Captain."

"We still don't know if Old Grouch is a thief. He might be trying to get some family jewels past customs officers without paying duty. On the other hand he might be involved in something much bigger."

"First we must find out what the diamond is worth. I don't know how to tell its value but we could ask Mr. Mc-Dermitt," said Lexie.

"If it's worth a lot he might ask some questions we couldn't answer."

"Well we can't tell the truth right now, it might spoil everything. We can't say we stole it from someone we think is a thief. Let's hurry to the jeweler's. I'll make up something if I have to until we can give the complete story. Let's go."

Mr. McDermitt examined the diamond Lexie handed him. He made a noise indicating his appreciation. "I don't work with such beauties. There are several skilled craftsmen I could recommend in New York. I should talk with your mother though. You shouldn't be carrying this around in your pocket! I'll give you a receipt for it. Please bring your mother back for it as soon as possible."

Lexie picked up the receipt and said, "Thanks. We'll be back very soon."

As soon as they were outside the store Lexie turned to Bill and said, "Come on! Let's go back and get the collar."

Now it seemed that all three thousand passengers had crowded onto the decks to recover from the storm. Trying to remain polite and get to the Upper Deck as quickly as possible became very difficult. Some of the passengers didn't understand English. "We should have learned 'Excuse me! May I pass through? Please! Thank you! Pardon me!' in ten different languages before we left home," said Lexie.

At last they reached the Upper Deck and found themselves alone. Buddy barked a welcome. "We can't play yet," said Lexie. "We've got work to do but we'll be back very soon."

Lexie ran to the St. Bernard. She shrieked, "Bill! Bill! Come here. It's unbelievable."

All the dogs began to bark. "What on earth is the matter? Calm down Lexie. Quiet Buddy. All be quiet. Are you trying to attract everyone's attention?"

"It doesn't matter anymore," wailed Lexie. Tears clouded her eyes. "Look...the collar. It's gone."

Bill looked at the neck of the St. Bernard. "Who could have taken it? And why?"

Instead of the wide leather band, the dog now wore a slim leather collar like the ones available in the ship's store.

Lexie recovered from her disappointment quickly. "Well, I made move three. That's enough for today. I'll play with Buddy and go swim with Debby and Glen. I'll relax and be ready to go full steam ahead tomorrow. This gets more and more interesting. There are two days yet. I still have two moves."

~10~

The Warning

"WELL," SAID LEXIE," it took all morning for me to make my costume for the fancy dress parade this afternoon. Then we had lunch and I haven't had a single idea as to what I'll do next. Move three gave us something definite to go on, but now all I know is we don't know what that something is. Oh crummy!"

"Maybe we should share this with Debby and Glen. They may have some ideas and it might help to have them do some observing. You'd better not let Old Grouch see much more of you," said Bill.

"I did promise to let them in on the Old Grouch game," answered Lexie. "Let's tell them we're suspicious but not mention the collar yet. I'll take the photo of Old Grouch with me when we meet them at the parade. It begins in half an hour. We'd better hurry and get dressed or we'll be too late. At least your costume is easy to expand after the huge lunch you just ate."

"I've got to draw a cobra and a vulture on the forehead

of my mask," Bill explained. "I've already outlined the eyes with this blue felt-tip pen. It's fun to dress up as the Egyptian boy king but I don't think I'd have liked to be the real Tutankhamen. I think a boy needs more time for cricket before taking on the responsibilities of a kingdom. Hey! I'd be ready sooner if you'd give me a little help with this toilet paper. I can't have any gaps in the mummy bandages."

"If you keep still I'll help. Mummies don't move," said Lexie. She'd chosen to be a Raggedy Ann doll with a slight difference. Lexie planned to put everything on backward including the orange yarn hair, a face mask, and big shoes. When in front of the judges she had a little act to perform. Her mother had helped with the costume by changing a roll of red and white striped crepe paper into stockings and a blouse. Another roll of dark blue crepe paper made the tunic. It was decorated with small white cotton flowers held on with safety pins.

"I'm ready, little sister. How about you?"

"I'm ready as soon as I get these boots on backwards. They must point the same way as my mask. Well, I think that's it. You may have to help me on the stairs. I wonder what Debby and Glen will be?"

"Let's go and find out," said Bill.

They looked very strange together: a mummy guiding a Raggedy Ann who had a difficult job going up the stairs.

Lexie said, "Remind me not to sit down. That would spoil things. Also ask Neptune to cooperate. I'm having enough problems thinking out how to react backwards."

"Hey!" exclaimed Bill. "I see a clown and a robot. They look the right height to be Glen and Debby.

Bill let go of Lexie's arm. He waved his arms around and

let out some weird groans and said, "I'm Tutankhamen come back to claim the jewels stolen from my tomb."

The robot laughed. "You didn't fool me for a minute, Bill. You'd better watch out in case someone sends you back to King Tut's tomb and seals you in."

"Okay, Glen. You didn't fool me either."

Lexie threw her arms out sideways to get their attention. She clapped her hands over her head three times. Then she bent to touch her knees and her toes. Of course it looked as if she bent backwards and touched her heels.

Some giggles came from the clown. "You look good, Lexie. That's neat."

"Thanks Debby," said Lexie. "If you'll come around behind me I can take a look at you."

The Deck Steward came over just then. He carried a tray of snacks. "How about some squash, biscuits, and sweets?" he inquired.

"Ick," said the clown.

"Sorry," said the Steward, "maybe I should have asked, 'How about some orange juice, cookies, and candy?'"

"That sounds more appetizing," said Debby.

"It's the same food. Only the language is different," said the Steward.

"I can't have any," said Lexie. "I can't let anyone see me eating through my hair."

The Deck Steward looked puzzled but walked on to the next group of children. "Why did you say 'ick' when the Steward offered you a snack, and then you took it and ate and drank all of it?"

"Well," answered Debby, "squash is a vegetable. We eat it and biscuits at dinner."

"Oh dear!" said Lexie. "I'm not looking forward to going to school in America. How will I know what the kids are talking about when the same words are used for different things?"

"You'll catch on little sister. Remember what Tom said?"

"Okay. Okay. Big brother. While you stuff yourself I'll tell Debby and Glen about the OG game. Take the photo out of my pocket. Got it? That's the man we call Old Grouch, OG for short."

"He's the one who hurt Buddy," observed Debby.

"Right," answered Lexie. "We think he's up to something fishy. We mean to find out what it is before we reach New York. If you see him talking with anyone else or anything suspicious let us know."

The Deck Steward came back for their empty glasses. He glanced at the photo in Debby's hand then left the deck with his tray full of used dishes.

A lively march came over the public address system. It stopped after a few minutes and a voice announced, "All contestants are invited to follow the clown to the lounge where the judges are waiting to decide on the winners."

The music continued and a clown arrived carrying a huge bundle of balloons that he began to hand out to all the children in costume. Lexie had a hard time keeping up with the music. Fortunately she wouldn't have music when in front of the judges.

Bill came to the judges' table first. He groaned and claimed to be in search of the people who'd stolen the treasures from his tomb.

Lexie worked into her show slowly, hoping she gave the

illusion of being able to bend completely backwards to touch her heels.

The judges made notes.

The clown announced, "While the judges reach their decisions, a fortuneteller will read the palms of any contestants who would like to know what the future holds for them."

He pointed to a gypsy seated at a table with a crystal ball. Curtains gave some privacy and atmosphere. Lexie and Debby joined the line of children who wanted to hear what the gypsy would say. Bill and Glen weren't interested.

When Lexie's turn came she smiled and sat at the table as she held out her hand.

The gypsy looked first at Lexie then at her hand. The gypsy muttered, "Stay away from the man with a walking stick. Mind your own business or you'll come to a nasty end."

The smile left Lexie's face. Her turn was over and the gypsy was already beckoning to the next person who was also the last in line.

Lexie rushed over to Debby. "What did the gypsy tell YOU?" she asked.

Debby laughed, "She said I would meet a tall, handsome boyfriend! Do you think Bill comes under that description?"

At that moment the clown held up his hands for silence. Then he announced, "The judges have made their decisions. The winning girl is...Raggedy Ann." Clapping followed as Lexie walked backwards to claim her prize.

"The winning boy is...King Tut!" More clapping came from the other competitors.

When Bill and Lexie returned to the Robot and Clown,

Glen said, "Lexie, I always thought you were a prize-winning doll. The judges had to pick you."

Lexie glared at Glen through her carrot yarn hair.

Bill said, "That's not nice, Glen. You insulted my sister. You'd better apologize."

"For what?" asked Glen.

"You called her a doll and a prize winning one too!"

"So?"

"Wait a minute. Glen has that look on his face that Tom warned us about. Are you speaking different languages again?" asked Debby.

"How did I insult you, Lexie?" asked Glen.

"You called me a doll! Just pretty clothes and a painted face but NO BRAIN. You are very rude to speak to me like that!" said Lexie, still fuming.

"Oh! That's what you heard? To call someone a doll is a casual compliment in America. It means you're attractive. No reference to brains involved."

"Oh! That's different," said Lexie. "I'm going to need my brain. That gypsy gave me a warning to stay away from the man with a walking stick. That could only be Old Grouch. Now I have other questions. Who is the gypsy? Why did she give me that message?"

"I don't know," said Bill. "It's hot in this costume. I've got to get changed and get a snack. My brain doesn't work on an empty stomach."

~11~

Taking a Risk

"**D**EBBY AND GLEN ARE late for breakfast," said Bill.

"Debby's probably dreaming about the tall, handsome boyfriend she's going to meet. But this is the start of the fourth day. Nobody else came up with any suggestions yesterday. So I'm making my next move. I'm going to search OG's cabin for some clues. We've never seen Old Grouch with anybody else."

"I can't let my little sister go alone. I'll join you."

"Let's see if we can find him on any deck. If we see him in a deck chair we'll know his cabin's empty."

Bill moved in the direction of the Promenade Deck. Lexie followed him then suddenly whispered, "Crummy! He's right there by the funnel. See the Deck Steward covering him with a blanket? Old Grouch looks better. Let's hope he takes a nice long rest. Jolly good. Let's hurry."

They walked quickly and calmly to level B.

"Here goes," said Bill as they arrived at OG's room. He knocked firmly on the cabin door.

There was no answer. Lexie turned the handle very slowly and opened the door. Bill signaled to Lexie to stand back. He walked inside. No one was there. He called to Lexie, "Come on in, close the door and get started looking for clues." Bill opened the closet and quickly ran his hands down the clothes and felt in all the pockets. Then he went through the three drawers in the chest being very careful to leave the few things as if undisturbed.

Lexie didn't touch a thing. She looked around the room. She saw a small poster about a dog show in New York. The date for that was a few weeks after they were due to land in New York. Then she saw the dog magazine Old Grouch had been reading in the lounge.

"Bill," said Lexie, "do you realize that if Old Grouch is traveling with a valuable dog already registered to enter an important dog show, we would have to have some very definite evidence to shake his story. I do know that dog isn't his." Suddenly her ears noticed a familiar sound on the hardwood floor of the corridor. The tap...tap...tap of the man with the walking stick and something else. Another person. They were talking. "He's coming," she whispered frantically. "I'm getting under the bed. Be quick... .there's room for you. Shhh."

As Bill rolled under the bed the door of the cabin opened. Lexie heard the door close. "Don't you lock your door?" a male voice questioned.

"No need to. I carry all my valuables with me. Come here if you want to see something bea-u-ti-ful." Old

Grouch walked over to the bed followed by the other man. This kept Bill on edge since their feet extended under the bed and he had to dodge them as they moved and changed places going from one end of the bed to the other.

Lexie had heard a little noise but couldn't identify what had made that sound. She thought, They are looking at something very special on that bed.

"Whew!" said the unknown man. "You're right. They are booty. And your stick was full. So right you are mate. They are bootyfull."

"If I get what I think these gems are worth you won't need to help me any more. We can both retire early. You see, I don't need to lock my door and have the inconvenience of having to find my key. I carry these gems in my stick at all times. It is attached to me so that I can't leave it somewhere accidentally. When I go to sleep it is in bed with me or in a deck chair. I sewed this leather band myself and it won't be removed until I get to the fence in New York. That last actress had so much I couldn't get it all in my stick so I made a wide, double collar for the dog and put the rest of the gems between the layers of leather."

The unknown person asked, "When do I get my share? I need some cash."

"I'm expecting a ship-to-shore message before I can answer you," said Old Grouch. "Meet me at lifeboat station ten at ten o'clock tomorrow night. Everybody else will be at last night parties by that time and it will be almost dark."

"Well I hope so, but why don't we discuss things now while we're sure no one else is around. I've still got a few minutes left for my tea break."

"There's nothing to discuss! Certainly not! Definitely not! Absolutely not!"

"Well I want a discussion!"

"I think I made it perfectly clear. I make the decisions. Don't come to my cabin ever again. We must not be seen together. Certainly not. Definitely not. Absolutely not!"

"Okay! You've always been fair. Tonight at ten at lifeboat ten."

Lexie listened as the cabin door opened. She hoped Bill could see who went out.

Bill didn't move so she guessed only one person left. Then she heard some small noises above her. She guessed Old Grouch must be putting the jewels back in the hollow walking stick. Next she thought he walked to the door, opened it and left. Then the tap, tap, tap faded.

"Golly," said Bill eventually. "We'd better wait a little while. We MUST make sure he isn't in the corridor. Things are worse than I thought."

Lexie said, "I can't wait to get out from under this bed. Now I'll have claustrophobia for the rest of my life. I'm so cramped. My legs are numb."

"Who was the other man?" asked Bill.

"I've heard his voice before," said Lexie.

"Yes. Where? When?"

"I have to get out of here and think somewhere else!"

"It should be safe now. Oooh! I'm stiff too. We'd better go for a swim. For the rest of the day we'd better wander around the ship and concentrate on voices. It wasn't George or Ben or Tom. Who else have we heard?"

"We can't tell Debby and Glen until tomorrow night. We don't know enough yet to explain why we were in Old

Grouch's room. We'd better go swimming and work out the kinks in our muscles and hope Debby and Glen come to the pool later because we'd better not explain to anyone why we feel so stiff," said Lexie. "Then I'm going to groom Buddy so he will be the most beautiful dog to arrive in the New World. I need something to take my mind off waiting for tomorrow night. I've only got one move left for checkmate with Old Grouch in five moves. Crummy!"

~ 12 ~

Last Night at Sea

L EXIE, BILL, DEBBY, AND GLEN had just finished their last dinner on board.

"We have a temporary place to stay arranged by my dad's new boss," said Lexie. "We only have our email addresses. Do you get email?"

"Sure, here's my card. I designed it myself," she said and passed it to Lexie. "It will be fun to meet again. On weekends we could visit the famous tourist spots. There are so many of them. Also I'm giving you an invitation to join our youth group. You wouldn't win our New Year prize for the resident who traveled the most miles from their homeland or the prize for the one who speaks fluently in the most languages unless you know more than seven. Also I doubt you'd get the prize for knowing the most poets, writers, artists, photographers, or playwrights from all the countries around the world. Bill might win that one."

Lexie asked, "Is there an award for knowing the most dances from all the countries around the world?"

"No," replied Debby, "but I'll bring that up when I get back. That would definitely be valid in our multi-cultural group. Since this is August there just may be something by January. Every culture has music, poetry, dance, and literature. We share our similarities although we express our creativity in different ways."

Lexie replied, "My mother has spent her life collecting and teaching dances from all over the world. She has taught me all she knows. So I might surprise you by winning an award for dance."

Debby said, "I hope so. Perhaps your mother would be willing to teach the rest of us some dances."

Bill said, "You know, I'm feeling sad that this journey is nearly over."

"It isn't over yet," said Glen. "A lot can happen in the next few hours."

"I hope too much doesn't happen," said Lexie with great feeling.

Lexie and Bill's parents arrived to start their dinner. "It has been such a restful journey, dear," Mother said to Father. "It has been lovely to have a week with nothing I must do. To have someone else prepare all the food, do all the dishes, and plan things for us and the children has been a true vacation. I do hope you young people haven't been bored. Have you?"

"Not a dull moment, Mum, I mean Mom. Boy! We're so close to America I'd better speak the language," said Bill.

"Lexie seems lost in her own thoughts again," observed Father. "Have you enjoyed the trip, Lexie?"

"Oh...yes...Dad, " answered Lexie, coming back to the present from her imaginings about what would be revealed at ten o'clock at lifeboat ten. "I'm so glad we came by ship. It wouldn't seem like we were going to another country if we'd gone by jet and arrived in five hours."

Mother said, "We may be more tired than when we left England. We'll be at the ball until midnight enjoying a social evening with the new friends we've made on board. We have to be up on deck at 3:00 a.m. if we want to see the Statue of Liberty and the famous Manhattan skyline. We don't want to miss anything on our arrival in what will be our New World. And I do want to take you into the ballroom later this evening so that you can see how adults make a special night of dancing and being sociable."

"I'd love that," said Lexie. "I bet the ladies will be wearing gorgeous dresses."

"Oh. Yuck! Girl stuff," said Bill. Then he looked at his new watch. "Lexie, it's time for us to feed Buddy if we're going to get EVERYTHING done tonight."

Lexie got the significance of his message and stood up. She hoped she looked calmer than she felt. As they left the dining room Lexie asked, "Bill how could you eat so much tonight of all nights. My stomach is full of butterflies."

"Come on, stupid. If you'd eat enough the butterflies would get squashed. We've got to get hidden. We'll take care of Buddy later."

"Don't you think we should tell someone what we know already?" asked Lexie.

"No. Not yet. We've come this far. We have to see it

through. It would be our word against Old Grouch and we don't know who his accomplice is at the moment. Do you want me to go alone?"

"No way! This is MY last move. I'm scared but I won't back out now. You'll have to wait a minute. While we're near the ballroom I'm going to peek inside."

"Oh!" said Lexie when she saw the decorations. "I wish I was a grownup and could go to the ball. Come and look Bill. There are glass chandeliers, red velvet drapes, and all the many large mirrors have gilt frames. The chairs have red velvet seats and backs. Come on, Bill. Look! You'll be a grownup yourself one day. If you have a wife or a young lady you hope will become your wife, she'll want to go out somewhere special for anniversaries and birthdays. You won't be able to say, 'Yuck. Girl stuff.'"

"Oh! All right! I looked," said Bill, after he poked his head around the door for one second.

"Boys!" said Lexie, poking her tongue out at him.

Bill dragged Lexie away from the door. "Hurry or we'll be too late to hide," he pointed out.

"Okay. I am going as fast as I can," said Lexie. She heard music. "Oh! That's a waltz I recognize. While the adults dance the children have a party so of course there are no people around. We must be nearly there. Yes. I see lifeboat number nine.

"This is it, Sis, number ten. Climb up on the seat and help me loosen the tarp. Hold on to the post and lower yourself into the boat."

"I hope it is as easy to get out as it is to get in," said Lexie as she scrambled for the middle seat in the lifeboat.

Bill stood on the seat and almost vaulted into the boat

barely touching the post. "Okay," he said. "We must ease the tarp over the edge of the lifeboat and we can raise it just a little to look out. No one will look up here. Settle down as comfortably as you can and wait in silence."

* * * *

Meanwhile Mother and Father had returned to their cabin to get dressed for the dance.

Father said, "I thought Bill had turned over a new leaf. He was so keen to use my razor blade during the storm. He wanted to mend his camera case, but look at it there, all forgotten. I thought it unusual for Bill to mend anything."

"The children were probably at loose ends during the storm," answered Mother. She put on her gold earrings as the final touch to her appearance for the ball. Her gold, iridescent long gown made a wonderful change from the tennis shoes and pants of the previous five days.

"You're beautiful, dear," said Mr. Costa. "Those earrings are the perfect touch. I thought I married a sensible woman. And you're beautiful too. Cinderella couldn't have appeared more glamorous at the ball."

"Well you quite outdo Prince Charming. It isn't very often that I see my husband in a tuxedo and patent leather shoes. I'm proud to have you as my escort."

Before they could exchange any more thoughts on the subject they heard a knock on the cabin door. When Mr. Costa opened it a man greeted him with,

"Hi. I'm John McDermitt from the jewelry shop. I'm looking for Lexie Costa."

"You've come to the right place," said Father. "Is there a problem?"

"No. You have two very nice children. The only problem is Lexie's a little forgetful. She brought this diamond to me and I gave her a receipt, but I asked her to bring her mother back to claim it. I thought I could recommend someone in New York to Mrs. Costa if she wanted to get a new setting for her ring. Lexie had it in her pocket and I wondered if you are as unaware of its value as your daughter. I didn't want her to drop it somewhere."

He handed a small ring size box to Mrs. Costa. She opened the box and a surprised look showed on her face. She handed the box to her husband. He frowned and asked, "Where did Lexie say she got this?"

"Well...she didn't! I just assumed it belonged to her mother. I didn't ask any questions."

Father said, "I expect the children are already at their party in the lounge. Let's go and find them and get this sorted out. I expect some lady on this ship is frantic thinking she lost the diamond from her ring. Since this is the last night we must sort this out quickly and notify Lost Property immediately. We'll come to your shop as soon as we find Lexie and get her explanation about the diamond."

~13~

Bad Luck

BILL RAISED THE TARP slightly and looked at his watch for the twentieth time. Ten o'clock. He nodded to Lexie and gave a thumbs up sign. Before they saw anyone the tap, tap, tap on the hardwood decks told them who was coming. The tapping soon stopped because Old Grouch sat on the bench below them. Moments later the Deck Steward appeared carrying a blanket.

"Slightly chilly tonight, isn't it, Sir?" he inquired.

"Cut out the nonsense," snapped Old Grouch.

"It's better, Sir, if I look as if I'm taking care of your needs, just in case someone comes along for a romantic walk in the moonlight."

Lexie thought, *So this is why I knew his voice. It's Jack, the Deck Steward. He served us a snack at the fancy dress parade and he must have been watching and listening while I showed the picture of OG to Debby and Glen. Then Jack changed into the gypsy costume and disguised his voice to warn me to stay away from Old Grouch.*

"Let's get on with it," said Old Grouch. "Here's the phone number of our contact in New York. Once we are off the ship our only contact is through him"

"When do I get my cut? I told you I need money."

"I don't get any pay until we return to England. You get one-third of all profit for giving me a copy of the names and addresses of first class passengers leaving New York and Southampton to cruise the Atlantic. I get two=thirds because I do all the investigations and the actual robbery and working with a fence on both sides of the Atlantic. This last haul is so good the gems might be too hot to sell for a while even in new settings. On this trip the owners of that dumb St. Bernard pay my passage. It also gives me a wonderful alibi. While I have to wait for the dog to get out of quarantine and then take it to the dog show, I get plenty of time to check out the homes of the passengers who leave on the next trip to Southampton. If they're so dumb as to leave without a house sitter or to take their fabulous jewelry to a safety deposit box before they leave the country, don't blame me for their stupidity. While Scotland Yard is in hot pursuit of a thief in England, I'm cruising on my way to New York with the evidence. When the NYPD are searching for a thief in the USA, I'm cruising again on my way to England with the booty."

Lexie thought, *So that's how they do it. A couple of crooks working together.* She looked at Bill who was holding up the tarp and shook her head in amazement at Old Grouch's story. She forgot where she was for a moment and stretched a little. She carelessly knocked an oar with her elbow. It hit the bottom of the lifeboat with a thud.

"What was that?" asked Old Grouch.

"An oar or something slipped in the lifeboat," said Jack.

"Check it! We can't afford mistakes. Why would an oar or anything else suddenly slip?"

Jack swung himself up to the lifeboat via the support post, pulled back the tarpaulin and saw two very frightened children who'd overheard all the thieves' plans. He recovered from his surprise very quickly and grabbed Bill's ankles as he called to Old Grouch, "Two kids here. Grab the girl's arms and twist them. I've got the boy."

Jack turned towards Lexie and Bill. "Now listen, both of you, not one sound from either of you. If the boy makes any noise he will get to watch me throw the girl overboard. Then I'll throw him over. If the girl makes a noise she can watch while I throw the boy overboard. Then she'll get the same watery grave. Is that clear? It's dark and everyone is partying. No one will know. Your obituaries will read 'LOST AT SEA.' Do you understand? I warned you to stay away from the man with a stick. Now you are in trouble."

Lexie was surprised at the strength of Old Grouch when he grabbed her. She dared not make any noise. Jack tied Bill's feet and hands together with rope already stored in the lifeboat. Then the Steward reached for the first aid supplies. Lexie watched with a feeling of horror as he pushed a roll of bandage into Bill's mouth, then sealed his mouth with a square of adhesive. The Deck Steward turned and repeated everything with Lexie. Her legs were tied together at the ankles. Then she was gagged. When her hands had been tied together, another rope was used to tie Lexie and Bill back to back. Then Old Grouch and Jack lowered them to the bottom of the boat.

Old Grouch said, "I have a limp but I'm not helpless. My arms are like iron bands."

Lexie had been amazed that Old Grouch used the pole and got into the boat as easily as Bill. Lexie thought, *I wish Mervin the Magician had taught us the secret for getting out of tied ropes.* Then Jack tied Bill and Lexie back-to-back across the lifeboat.

Old Grouch and Jack pulled the tarpaulin back over the lifeboat and left Lexie and Bill in the dark. Jack jumped down to the seat and Old Grouch lowered himself down the post.

Old Grouch snorted, "Why'd they have to poke their noses into other people's business? What brats! Children should be kept in their own cabins. They should not be on decks or in restaurants or lounges or lifeboats. Certainly not! Definitely not! Absolutely not!"

Jack, who had resumed his position as the helpful Deck Steward, asked, "And now, Sir, what do we do about the kids, Sir?"

Old Grouch answered, "They heard everything. We'll just have to wait until it's completely dark, then throw them overboard."

Jack said, "Now just a minute. I agreed to help steal jewels from wealthy passengers who leave their treasures unguarded while they're away from home, but I'm not getting mixed up with drowning two children."

"You don't have to. I'll come back and do it myself. Don't forget our agreement. You get a third for supplying me with addresses of first class passenger. I check their houses for jewelry. I get two-thirds because I do any and all work needed. I've never let you down have I?"

"I never thought it would come to this! I can't go along with murder! Why don't we leave them tied up and gagged? We dock in the morning. All lifeboats have to be checked before the ship returns. The kids will be found hungry, thirsty, and upset, but not hurt."

"They'd report us to the authorities. Let me handle this. I told you if we get the price I hope for on the gems we can both retire in comfort and never have to do it again."

Lexie heard footsteps approaching. Then she heard her mother ask, "Have you seen a fourteen-year-old boy with a twelve-year-old girl? The boy has fair hair and the girl is a brunette. They were supposed to be at the party but they aren't there."

Jack replied, "No children have been up here tonight. I'm sure all children are at the party. They wouldn't miss it. So much is planned for their last night of fun while the adults are at the ball."

"Some fun we're having," thought Lexie wishing she could move an oar or anything else right now.

"We've tried *everywhere*," she heard her father say, emphasizing the everywhere.

Then to her surprise Lexie heard Mr. McDermitt's voice. He said, "It's odd we can't find them. You see, Jack, the girl found a very expensive diamond. Her parents want to get the gem back to its owner and now they're alarmed to be unable to find their children."

"The children are probably in a friend's cabin. Don't worry. They'll turn up. Just take the gem to the lost property office. Get a receipt. If it isn't claimed it will be yours and you can get it set in a ring," advised the Deck Steward.

"Thank you and goodnight," Lexie heard her father say. Then she heard several pairs of feet walk away. She wished she could do something to attract her parents' attention. She couldn't even kick the boat or bang her head on the side or bottom due to being tied back to back with Bill.

Then she heard Old Grouch speak again. "Things are more complicated. While you were talking and guiding those parents away, I was thinking. The only thing with diamonds in it that has been out of my sight is the dog's collar. I just checked it. Take a look."

"It looks all right to me," answered Jack. "What's the problem?"

"Look near the buckle. Somebody has cut the stitches.... and feel here...there's a space. Somebody has removed one gem. Guess who? How did those two no-good kids decide to hide in this particular lifeboat? We only spoke about this once, when we were in my cabin! So these two brats that you want to shelter must have been hiding in my cabin. Why? Do you STILL want to protect the little darlings?"

"You could throw the dog collar and the walking stick overboard and we'd just have to count this job as a loss. There'd be no evidence. Who'd believe a couple of kids? You have the dog as an alibi and I work on this ship. I've covered you with a blanket just once."

"I couldn't throw these beautiful gems in the ocean. Certainly not! Definitely not! Absolutely not! What a dreadful waste. Gems like this are rare. And kids? Bah! Everyone knows the world is over populated. Besides, it may save their parents a lot of heartache to lose them now before the brats start with teenage problems. I had three kids myself. When I got hurt on my job and had to take a small disability pension, my generous darlings sent me one 'Sorry You're Sick' card. Bah! Kids!"

"I'm sorry your children turned out to be so thoughtless, but because of them I can't hurt those two up there. If they don't show up, the Captain will have this ship crawling with police and nobody will be allowed to leave once we get to the pier."

Lexie hoped Jack would win the argument, although for the first time she did feel some sympathy for Old Grouch. Now she knew his limp was real and the cause of much sadness in his life. Perhaps he was so cross because of his bitterness or perhaps he was in constant pain. Lexie's thoughts were interrupted.

"Don't worry about a thing," Old Grouch said. "Just make sure we aren't seen together until we meet in New York. On second thought, we'd better not meet even in New York. Here's the phone number of our fence. We will have to go at separate times. We mustn't mess up our early retirement. Now go!"

Lexie heard no tap, tap, tap but only footsteps getting farther away. So Old Grouch must still be sitting below them. She could hear the ocean waves, and the ship's engines, and music from the ballroom. She felt remorse. How clumsy of her to move that oar. She wished she could talk with Bill. She wished someone had talked with OG's children. Most of all she wished she could get untied.

Well, wishing won't get me out of this mess, thought Lexie. *I must figure out what I can do. First I must get this tape off my mouth so that I can call out if anybody comes this way.* With difficulty she rubbed her left cheek repeatedly against the bottom of the boat to make a beginning on removing the adhesive across her mouth. She hurt her cheek from the friction. Her shoulder muscles ached. Her mouth remained sealed. She realized she would have to rest and then repeat the process over and over and over again.

After some time, Lexie heard a message over the public address system: "This is your Captain speaking. Mr. and Mrs. Costa are trying to locate their children. Bill is fourteen. He has blue eyes and fair, slightly curly hair. Lexie is twelve. She has long, straight brown hair and brown eyes. Many of you probably know them since they helped with the dog show and the magic show. Anyone who has seen them since they left the restaurant after dinner tonight please come to the office and let the Purser know.

Lexie thought, *Old Grouch and the Deck Steward are the only ones who've seen us. Will Jack tell?*

Lexie guessed another half-hour had passed. Every muscle in her body complained. Her cheek felt raw but she ignored that. She had made some progress. A little adhesive had curled back. She knew she must focus her attention on removing the gag.

"This is your Captain speaking," came over the public address system again. "All stewards are to report to the office. All passengers are to return to their cabins. I'm sorry to interrupt the festivities but the Costa's children, Lexie and Bill, are still missing. This is serious. A complete search of this ship will be made. Stewards will be coming to all cabins. Nobody is to leave his or her cabin until I give the word."

Lexie heard the tap of Old Grouch's stick as he left, presumably for his cabin. She had continued making progress on the adhesive. She knew if she could push that bandage out of her mouth with her tongue she'd be able to make a noise of some kind. Although every part of her body hurt she knew she had to focus on being able to yell. Her patience paid off. The adhesive still hung on the right side of her mouth but she'd removed enough. Now she hoped gravity would help her tongue remove that bandage before she gagged. Eventually she called quietly, "Bill, I can yell next time we hear someone. I hope someone comes soon. My shoulder is numb, I've got pins and needles in my leg, and the wood in this boat gets harder by the minute."

Old Grouch answered a knock on his cabin door. He almost got knocked over because Jack, the Deck Steward, came in so quickly.

"What are you doing here you fool? I told you we must not be seen together," snapped Old Grouch.

"You don't give all the orders," Jack stated. "I'm supposed to be searching the deck in my usual work area. If the kids aren't found the Captain is going to change the areas to be searched by each steward. It's going to look funny if I miss a couple of kids in a lifeboat on my own deck. I have to be the one to find them. Give me the jewels. I'll toss them overboard. Then I'll go and discover the kids!"

"No! Certainly not! Definitely not! Absolutely not! When the Captain calls the stewards back, and while the new search areas are being worked out, I'll cut the rope where you tied the kids together and toss them over one at a time. They'll go straight to the bottom of the Atlantic. I'm the one in charge of our retirement. Now get out."

Meanwhile in lifeboat number ten, Lexie listened carefully. She only heard the ocean and ship noises. "Somebody must be coming to search the other side of this deck. There are too many lifeboats, restrooms, and lounges for one steward's watch," she said. "I'm ready to scream louder than OG did when he fell overboard."

After about another half-hour she heard, "This is your Captain speaking. Everyone stay in your cabins. All stewards will be assigned to different areas of the ship and different stewards will come to every cabin, lounge, store, restroom, etc. The children have not been found."

~14~

Checkmate

BEN THE KENNEL STEWARD heard the Captain's second call. He delayed a few moments. He muttered to the dogs, "They've never missed feeding Buddy before. I can't understand it. I'd better give him something myself."

He heard footsteps and turned to see Debby and Glen. Debby said, "I know we're supposed to be in our cabin but we're so worried about Lexie and Bill. Then we remembered what Lexie said at the dog show. Remember? She said Buddy could always find her. Please let Buddy out. Then we can take him on every deck. He'll find them."

Ben said, "It's worth a try. Come on, Buddy. Find Lexie. Find Bill." Buddy ran off toward the stairs. Debby, Glen, and Ben followed.

Lexie listened carefully. Soon after the Captain's second call she was relieved to hear someone coming. "This must be the person coming to search the deck," she said to Bill. She smiled and was about to yell HELP, but just as she opened her mouth, her ears picked up a familiar and most unwelcome sound: the tap, tap, tap of a walking stick. Her heart began to pound so hard it hurt her chest. "It must be dark by now, Bill. Old Grouch is coming to throw us overboard. Have you managed to get any ropes loosened? I guess not or you would be helping me out of mine. I think we've been tied up with sailors' knots."

The tap, tap, tap got closer, then too close. Her blood pounded in her ears. She felt faint. Her head hurt. Suddenly she remembered her whistle. *If I can reach it with the help of my shoulder, teeth and tongue Buddy might draw attention by barking until he is allowed out of the kennel.* She maneuvered the whistle gradually toward her mouth until she could grasp it securely in her teeth. She couldn't hold her whistle with her fingers as she did at the show. It was difficult to hold it with her lips while she blew and blew. She couldn't hear if it worked. When she realized the tapping had stopped she told herself, "Be calm. Blow again! Blow again!"

The noise of tarpaulin being untied and wrinkled made her break out in a sweat. Then the ship's lights filled the boat with soft yellow light. It was not too brilliant a change from the darkness her eyes had been used to for so long. Now she thought, "When I see Old Grouch I'm going to faint. At least I'll be unconscious when I hit the water."

Now her blood pounded so loudly in her ears she heard nothing else. Then she did hear Old Grouch yell, "Oh! Another dumb dog!"

Then she heard a familiar bark. Buddy barked and

barked. "Someone let Buddy out, Bill. I hope that some-one is very close since Buddy can't untie the ropes."

Now I don't know what is happening. I can only see the sky. Now there is a sound I can't identify.

The rest of the tarpaulin was pulled off completely. Lexie closed her eyes, dreading what would happen next.

"What are you two doing here?" asked Ben's friendly voice. She heard a fast tap, tap, tap of Old Grouch's walking stick fading into the distance.

Lexie opened her eyes and saw Ben. She was so close to tears she couldn't speak. Buddy continued to bark. Debby and Glen came running, yelling, "Good Buddy. Good Buddy."

Ben took over. "Glen, break the glass on that emergency phone. Tell the Captain to come to lifeboat station ten immediately and to bring Mr. and Mrs. Costa. Say their children are safe. You get back here fast and help with Lexie and Bill. Can you pass Buddy up here first? Hurry."

Buddy wagged his tail and licked Lexie then Bill. All three were happy to be reunited.

Ben removed the adhesive and bandage from Bill's mouth and then the adhesive hanging from Lexie's mouth. As Ben cut the ropes he said, "Debby rub Lexie's legs. Perhaps Lexie can rub her own arms. I'll help Bill."

"Thanks," Bill tried to say but his mouth was too dried out from fear and the gag. "It was Debby's idea to let Buddy out to find you," said Ben as he continued to rub Bill's sore limbs. When you feel able to, sit on the seat and see how you are there before you attempt to stand up. I want to know who tied you up, but that must wait until your parents arrive."

Glen returned followed almost immediately by the three adults.

Mother screamed, "What happened?" when she saw her disheveled children. "Was this some child's idea of a prank?" asked Father.

Lexie answered, "The Deck Steward and the owner of the St. Bernard tied us up." Bill, trying to work some saliva around his mouth, wasn't able to speak yet.

The Captain said, "We'll hear all the explanations later. First let's go to my cabin to relax and have some refreshments. I'll call the ship's doctor. This has been a traumatic experience for all concerned."

Lexie and Bill were helped out of lifeboat number ten. Mother walked with her arm around Lexie. Buddy walked at her side. Father linked his arm in Bill's. Once in the comfort of the Captain's cabin and supplied with a choice of cold water, hot chocolate, tea, and a large piece of chocolate cake, everyone soon felt improved. Buddy had a special plate of treats and curled up happily on the rug.

The doctor arrived and attended to Lexie's raw cheek. Then he listened to the heartbeats of Lexie and Bill. They had elevated pulses but the doctor said, "That's no surprise. I'd have a rapid heart beat if I'd been through what you've been through. I'll keep an eye on you but I expect your pulses will slowly return to normal. By tomorrow you won't be much the worse for wear. Call me at any time during the night if I'm needed. I'll see that young lady's cheek again in the morning."

"I don't want to rush you," said the Captain, "but we're all interested in the explanation. I have a detective on board and I'll call him. Next I'll call Debby and Glen's parents to put their minds at rest and see if they'll allow Debby and Glen to stay here for the rest of the night with you. Finish up the cake and have more to drink while I make the phone calls."

Lexie said, "Please ask George if his German Shepherd, Hans, can help get the evidence."

"I'll check that out with the detective first. We must be very careful to follow the laws and not let the criminals get off because we blunder in collecting the evidence and getting them to the proper authorities," said the Captain. "Excuse me for a few minutes."

By the time the Captain finished his second phone call there was a knock at the door. A tall, powerful man entered. "This is Ted. He's a detective," the Captain announced. "Now, Bill and Lexie, you can begin."

"It's really Lexie's story," said Bill, with his mouth full of chocolate cake. "I didn't believe her until she showed me the diamond. I teased her about her vivid imagination."

"All my hunches weren't correct," said Lexie. "I was right about Old Grouch—that's our name for Mr. Sanders—having something to hide. I didn't even suspect the Deck Steward. I don't think he is quite such a bad man as Old Grouch. He wanted some easy money but he didn't want to throw us overboard. He tried to get Old Grouch to throw the jewels in the ocean and get rid of the evidence because no one would believe a couple of kids. It was Bill's idea to follow up my suspicions and we found out that Old Grouch stole regularly from first-class passengers traveling on this ship. The Deck Steward's part was to supply their names, addresses, and departure dates from New York and Southampton."

Mother and Father listened in astonishment as Lexie and Bill recounted the events leading up to their capture and eventual rescue.

Bill said, humbly, "I have to take back what I said about you being dumb, Lexie. I've just realized I can remember things I read about better than you can, and I read a lot more. But you know things about people and animals that you can't read about anywhere."

Lexie glowed. She hadn't known she'd have to go through so much to win the admiration of her brother. "If it hadn't been for you, Bill, I wouldn't have found out the whole story. I would have been satisfied with the collar."

The Captain stood up and said, "I have to contact the New York Police Department. I've already had photographs taken of the lifeboat, the ropes we cut off of you, the bandages and adhesive, and John McDermitt is printing the pictures right now."

Ted asked, "Where are the jewels?"

Father said, "I've got the single diamond that Lexie removed from the dog's collar." He showed it to the detective, who whistled on seeing that sparkling gem!

Lexie said, "The rest of the evidence is in Old Grouch's pocket inside the dog's collar and in the metal cane attached firmly to his wrist. If you ask George to bring his trained German Shepherd, Hans, the dog will hold Old Grouch without hurting him until you recover the evidence. George demonstrated that at the show."

Ted said, "I'm going to join your Captain and discuss this with the police and Scotland Yard. The villains must be arrested and read their rights, and we'll pick up the evidence ASAP."

They had time to talk, answer questions, eat, and drink. Soon they heard an announcement on the intercom. "This is your Captain speaking. The festivities may continue. Strike up the band. Lexie and Bill have been found!"

Cheers and clapping resounded through the ship as the passengers rushed from their cabins. The Captain returned. He said, "Both men have been arrested and are in custody. George had Hans convince Mr. Sanders to stay still while we cut the leather holding the walking stick to his wrist. He was so frightened he tossed the collar out of his pocket himself and said he'd never traveled on a ship with so many dumb dogs."

"Checkmate," whispered Lexie to Bill.

"Also NYPD has been in touch with Scotland Yard. There's a big reward for recovery of the gems," reported the Captain. "You'll be contacted on shore."

"I remember that the newspaper I saw Old Grouch reading had a police report. I didn't read it. I didn't think that would be humorous," said Lexie. "But OG laughed because he thought he'd outsmarted the police again."

The Captain interrupted, "Look ahead. Do you see three white flashes every eight seconds? That's the Ambrose Light at the entrance to New York Harbor, a sight that a captain of any vessel crossing the three thousand miles of the Atlantic Ocean is very pleased to see. Only fifteen more miles of ocean to go. Soon I'll rely on the Sandy Hook Pilots to take over the *Ocean Queen*.

"Do we stop at the Ambrose Light?" asked Lexie.

"No," the Captain replied. "A little farther on you'll see the steady white light of Sandy Hook Lighthouse, a National Historic Landmark. A pilot will be waiting to come on board. Then my duties are over. The Sandy Hook Pilot will take over the *Ocean Queen*. He'll take us through the harbor in about two and a half hours. He must reduce speed to prevent damage from our wake. For the final skilled work, about a mile from the end of our journey, the docking pilot boards. He'll get the *Ocean Queen* into the passenger pier."

"I'd like to be a docking pilot," said Bill.

"Well, start preparing while you're young. That's a highly skilled job. You'll need four years of college, seven years as an apprentice, followed by seven years as a Deputy Pilot. For now I'll have someone call you in time to see the Sandy Hook pilot come on board. Then all of you can join me on the bridge for a view of the Statue of Liberty and the famous Manhattan skyscrapers."

"Thanks," said Bill.

"Terrific!" answered Debby.

"Awesome!" said Glen.

"Crummy!" said Lexie. "That will be smashing!"

"Mr. and Mrs. Costa, please join us," said the Captain. "Excuse me now. I have a little more work to finish.

After he left Mother sighed, "Well I couldn't sleep after the stress of the disappearance of my children. I think my extra adrenaline will keep me awake for a week! Instead of sleeping it will be exciting to see the famous sights we've only seen in movies."

In the early morning light, on the bridge with the Captain, they had an uninterrupted view of the Statue of Liberty, the Manhattan skyscrapers, and the harbor night workers. The Captain provided them with a chart so that they could follow their progress through the Lower and Upper Bays of the New Jersey/New York Harbor. "Watch for the Verrazzano-Narrows Bridge at the beginning of Upper Bay. It is the tallest bridge in the Port at almost three hundred feet."

"Crummy," said Lexie. "That's almost as tall as St. Paul's Cathedral."

Other ships and boats whistled as the *Ocean Queen* approached. She whistled back. "Ladies of the ocean are considered polite to return a whistle," said the Captain.

They made one stop for the Docking Pilot to board.

"I hope life in the New World is not quite as exciting as our journey to it," said Lexie.

"So do I," said Bill.

"Woof! Woof!" added Buddy.

For half an hour they watched the tugs, directed by the pilot with radio communication, push and pull them to dock at the passenger terminal.

Lexie smiled as she saw the American flag being raised on the British ship as a sign of friendship with the host country. She'd already made new American friends. She smiled as she said, "I don't know why I felt so scared about moving to a new home and a new school. I already have the skills needed to make new friends. I'm glad Dad took that new job. Listen to the sea gulls calling, "Stay! Stay! Stay!"

Sources of Information

Cunard Line. In five days I crossed the approximately 3000 miles of the Atlantic on the *Queen Mary* from Southampton on the south coast of England to New York/New Jersey Harbor on the east coast of the USA.

Famous Harbors of the World, by Eugene F. Morgan, Sr. Commissioner of the Port of New York Authority.

Port of Southampton

National Park Service of New York Harbor (718-354-4551)

Sandy Hook's Importance to New Jersey/New York Harbor/Fort Ha

Sandy Hook Pilots Sandy Hook Lighthouse. A National Historic Landmark. Built in 1764 in New Jersey. http:/WEBLIGHTHOUSES/LHNJ.html

Ambrose Lightship is now a museum. Ambrose Light http:/uscg.mil/haq/g-cp/history

National Maritime Museum, Greenwich, England, where east meets west at the Prime Meridian, 0 Longitude, where tourists pose for photos with a foot in each hemisphere.

A globe or map to see the lines of longitude across the Atlantic.

Longitude by Dava Sorbel (for teen to adult readers) with historical maritime information and details of the famous clocks of John Harrison, now on view at the National Maritime Museum, England. Although John Harrison was cheated out of his monetary prize by the Astronomer Royal (he was head of the selection committee) for solving the problem of longitude and saving the lives of many sailors, history records John Harrison, an observant carpenter, as the winner of a clock that could keep accurate time despite the heat, cold, and movements of ships at sea, and keep GMT (Greenwich Mean Time) as a reference point for reckoning distance traveled daily.

Captain W. W. Sherwood, of the Sandy Hook's Pilots Association, shared information on the activities of commerce that occur during the two-and-a-half hour journey to the passenger dock in New York Harbor.

About the Author

MABEL WREN WAS BORN in London, England. When she was five years old her parents took her to see the *Mauretania 11*, known as "the largest vessel ever to navigate the Thames and use the Royal Docks," according to the Cunard Archives.

The docks were open to the public for the festive occasion. The ships coming in and out of London docks and permanently docked in or near the Thames were her visual aids for geography and history. The *President Peron* and the *Eva Peron* were beautiful white ships and she was awed at the sight of them even before she knew anything about the people whose names they bore.

When eight years old she decided to visit another country by ship when she grew up. She didn't know then that one day she would cross the Atlantic on the *Queen Mary* on her way to a new job.

But before she could travel she had to have a career. She studied and received her elementary teaching credential from London University. After teaching for five years in London she applied for a teacher-exchange position in the USA. She had to agree to go anywhere in America.

Her exchange was arranged with a first-grade teacher in Trinidad, California, on the coast, near the Oregon border. She could only find out the highest and lowest temperatures, annual rainfall, and population (two hundred!) for her new residence. She'd committed her savings to this new adventure and these facts did nothing to reassure her she'd made a wise investment.

She soon arrived in a beautiful, small fishing and logging community on the Pacific coast. Problems arose because when she spoke English the locals heard American English. When they spoke American English she heard English. When she heard all the parents were upset because she'd burn down the school, she knew they needed to talk. Relief swept the community when they learned she only wanted each student to carry a flashlight on the stage. She'd used the English word "torch".

Today she has retired to about three thousand feet in the coastal mountain range of Trinity County, California, where the deer, mountain lions, bears, and skunks have the right-of-way.

www.palomabooks.com

Made in the USA
Las Vegas, NV
21 December 2020